JAGGED EDGES & MOVING PARTS

Pete Mesling

Other Kingdoms Publishing, Seattle

ISBN-13: 978-0-578-67738-5

Cover design by: Elderlemon Design
Library of Congress Control Number: 2020906732
Printed in the United States of America

PUBLICATION HISTORY

PRAISE FOR PETE MESLING'S WORK

"Pete Mesling's *None So Deaf* gave me a serious dose of the creeps. Herein lies an assemblage of horrors that, when it isn't reminding you of Bradbury at his grimmest, will have you double-checking the locks and turning on all the lights. Wonderful stuff indeed."
—**Kealan Patrick Burke**, Bram Stoker Award-winning author of *The Turtle Boy*, *Kin*, and *Sour Candy*

"Reminiscent of the best and darkest work of David Morrell and Dan Simmons, the new collection by Pete Mesling, *None So Deaf*, crackles with malignant life and death. You can smell and taste these stories, which are written with a surgeon's eye for detail and a mortician's sense of drama. Highly recommended!"
—**Jay Bonansinga**, New York Times best-selling author of *The Walking Dead: Invasion* and *Self-Storage*

"We've got the genealogical report in on Pete Mesling. There's some Fredric Brown. Some Kafka. And even some Brautigan. But mostly there's Mesling. And that's 100% unique and original. As is *None So Deaf*, this memorable collection."
—**Mort Castle**, author of *Moon on the Water*, *New Moon on the Water*, and *Knowing When to Die*

"With his debut collection of mad scientists and classic monsters, childhood wonders twisted into nightmares, and *Twilight Zone*-style morality plays, Pete Mesling reminds us what's fun about horror—and adds serious chills along the way."
—**Norman Prentiss**, Bram Stoker Award-winner, author of *Invisible Fences*

"Claustrophobic and terrifying; you'll be holding your breath."
—*Rue Morgue*

"This is bizarre stuff."
—**Thomas F. Monteleone**, Bram Stoker Award-winning author of *The Blood of the Lamb* and *The Mothers and Fathers Italian Association*

"Flashes of darkness ... moments of the macabre captured like the snapshots of a scream ... or an impaling. Short, fast, and deadly moments of discovery!"

—**John Everson**, Bram Stoker Award-winning author of *Covenant* and *Sacrificing Virgins*

"Pete Mesling's *None So Deaf* explores the darkest regions of the human soul in readable tales that take no prisoners."
—**Nancy Kilpatrick**, *Nevermore!: Tales of Murder, Mystery & The Macabre*

"A terrific new author. His work is fresh and different."
—**John R. Little**, author of *Miranda*, *The Memory Tree*, and *Soul Mates*

"Lean and masterful prose. Buy this book."
—**Wayne Allen Sallee**, author of *The Holy Terror* and *Proactive Contrition*

"Pete Mesling's fiction is definitely the kind of old school horror I grew up with. Short, sharp shocks that touch on the fears we all have—stuff like claustrophobia, the anger of strangers, carnivals, spooky houses. Definitely give them a whirl!"
—**Paul Kane**, Bestselling and award-winning author of *Pain Cages*, *The Hellraiser Films & Their Legacy*, and *Lunar*

"Pete Mesling is a brawler of a writer. Whether his touch is light as a feather, like Bradbury, or a hard left hook, like Lansdale, he has you exactly where he wants you."
—**John Bruni**, author of *Tales of Questionable Taste*

"Pete Mesling's *None So Deaf* takes the reader on a whistle stop tour of American gothic, traditional and modern, with unsettling carnivals, kids breaking into decrepit houses on a dare, and corrupt preachers in the Wild West. Nasty new stings in the tail alternate with tilted perspectives on horror tropes for this box of entertainingly poisoned chocolates."
—**Narrelle M Harris**, *The Opposite of Life*

"Just when you think you know what's going to happen, Mesling pulls the rug out and down the trapdoor you fall, spiraling into expertly crafted nightmares. I'm already looking forward to Pete's next offering!"
—**Robert Essig**, author of *In Black*, *People of the Ethereal Realm*, and *Stronger than Hate*

"None So Deaf spans the horror spectrum from fearsome to fun in the spirit of *Skeleton Crew* and *Strange Highways*, making it a great read for any fan of the genre!"
—**Matt Hults**, Author of *Husk*

For Paul, who was there when these seeds were planted and has stayed for harvest time.

'Tis now the very witching time of night,
When churchyards yawn and hell itself breathes out
Contagion to this world. Now could I drink hot blood
And do such bitter business as the day
Would quake to look on.

HAMLET, ACT 3, SCENE 2

CONTENTS

ACKNOWLEDGEMENTS

You've read it a thousand times: No book is ever the work of only one person. Well, if it's true of novels, it's doubly true of short-story collections. Roughly half of the tales in *Jagged Edges & Moving Parts* are new, but the rest were picked up individually somewhere along the line by editors and publishers who saw something shiny enough in my prose to take a chance on it.

A shout out, then, to James Roy Daley of Books of the Dead Press, who published an earlier collection of mine; Mort Castle, not only for believing in my potential, but for putting his money where his mouth was; Cathy Buburuz, who has fled the literary scene now, I believe, but who made her mark, and gave this writer plenty to think about; Neil Baker, a gentleman editor who was more patient with me than he had any reason to be; Theresa Dillon and Marc Ciccarone of Blood Bound Books, who had the nerve to publish a story of mine that not many editors would have wanted to get within a country mile of; and Tom Moran, for publishing and illustrating some of my work, both in his sorely missed Black Ink Horror line of lavishly illustrated anthologies and elsewhere.

Special thanks also to the Horror Writers Association; Tom Monteleone and the gang at Borderlands Press Writers Bootcamp; all who have generously blurbed and reviewed my work; and the many fine writers with whom I have shared tables of contents over the years—especially Patrick Loveland, for giving a damn at the perfect moment. Getting to know these folks personally, on social media, and through their fiction, artwork, and poetry has been an honor.

Finally, I would like to extend a heartfelt tip of the hat to my readers. Publishing is like an electric circuit. The writer pushes the current through, but it's the reader who makes sure it completes its course. My battery is fully charged, I assure you, so here's to a lasting partnership.

—Pete Mesling
Seattle, Washington

THE THINGS WE TEACH OUR YOUNG

T he first thing Dennis noticed was that he couldn't see for shit. The second was that his face felt wet. His right hand brushed against his eyeglasses on the seat beside him. They were intact, so he slid them on. The trunk of a giant fir consumed most of the view through his decimated windshield, and when he looked down at his shirt front all he saw was red. Even in a post-traumatic state he was able to put two and two together. He'd fallen asleep while driving and damn near paid for it with his life.

The steering wheel had clamped down on his right thigh, but he was able to wriggle his leg free by pressing himself into the seat and remove himself from the vehicle. Once outside, it became obvious that his Bronco would never take him away from it all again. It had breathed its last. He turned to look up toward the road. Extricating himself from the cab had been child's play compared to the climb he had in front of him if he wanted to reach the highway.

But he did want to reach the highway, and climb he did, one agonizing step at a time. Twice he had to grip a branch of protruding foliage to get past a particularly steep patch, and dizziness almost sent him reeling more than once, but he made it to the top in one piece. When he got to the roadside, he looked back down into the ravine and saw that his two-toned white-and-tan Bronco must have rolled several times before having its clock stopped by the aged fir. It looked as if a giant had begun crushing the rugged vehicle in its fist, only to be called away before it could complete the job. It was not lost on Dennis that he could have ended up in worse shape himself. Much worse.

The night was dry and clear, accented more than lit by a crescent moon that hung at a lazy distance from the treetops. He'd never hitchhiked a day in his life, but what other options did he have? Patting his pockets he'd realized his phone was nowhere on his person. He glanced into the ravine again. No way was he climbing back down to grope around for his phone, which probably wouldn't draw a signal out in these woods even if he did find it.

He began walking slowly along the shoulder, but really he was listening for a vehicle, and if one came from the direction he was walking in, he'd want to hustle across to the other side before it reached him.

Before long, lights arced around a bend at his back, washing the road ahead of him from right to left. The sound of the engine was next. Something fairly big. A truck, probably. Hope swelled within him. It must get pretty lonely on the road when you're a trucker, he figured. Maybe luck was on his side now that it had had its fun with him.

His mind tried to tell his arm to hail the driver, but something didn't connect. Instead he stopped and turned toward the vehicle bearing down on him and hoped he looked more pathetic than frightening.

For a horrible moment he feared the truck was going to pass him by, roll around the bend fifty yards up the road and disappear into the night, the diminishing roar of its engine a taunt. But as though imagining the worst had produced a talismanic effect against it becoming his fate, the truck pulled onto the shoulder just beyond where he stood. It was a six-wheel box truck that had seen better days. Nothing on the rear gate indicated what it was hauling or who it belonged to, but some slow-working part of his brain thought there had been a faded logo on the side panel.

Not that it mattered. He needed a lift in a bad way. Any risk in sharing a cab with a stranger was small spuds compared to the risk of waiting for the next passerby. He wasn't sure he'd make it much longer without medical attention. A chill was on him, despite the pleasant summer night, and his left side hurt more than he liked. Was there also a slight tremble in his hands? He was damn sure thirsty, and that could become a serious problem before anything else did.

He shuffled toward the truck on feet like cinder blocks.

The logo hadn't been a figment of his imagination. *Ernie's Heating and Cooling Services* was emblazoned on the side, accompanied by the image of a sly little fucker tipping his hat like he'd just kissed your mom on the mouth and was daring you to make something of it. When Dennis pulled open the passenger door, the dome light illuminated a driver with dark skin, maybe thirty years old, maybe younger. The man didn't look in his direction. There was an impatient air to the way he sat there gripping the steering wheel and staring out the windshield.

"I've, uh, run into a spot of trouble," Dennis said.

"I can see that," the driver responded, still looking straight ahead. "Hop in. I could do with some company. I'll get you to the nearest hospital. Your car go off the road?"

"Thanks, I appreciate it. Yeah, let myself fall asleep at the wheel." He hauled himself into the cab, but it took every ounce of strength he had. "The accent. Is that Arabic?"

The man nodded. "I'm from Damascus originally. Studied in London. The name is Akram."

Finally he turned and gave Dennis a weak smile.

Dennis pulled the heavy door shut, and then silence reigned between them as Akram guided the truck back onto the road and coaxed it through its gears to full speed.

"Do *you* have a name?" Akram asked.

"Yeah, I have a name." He thought about leaving it there but decided to keep things civil. Just because he had opinions didn't mean he had to share them with every Jim, Tim, and Slim he came across. Or every Akram. "Dennis."

"I don't have a phone. No CB, either. A ride is going to have to do it."

"Yeah. Look, like I said, I appreciate the help, but I'm tired and beat up. I'm really not up for a lot of conversation."

"There are some wipes in the glove box, for your face. Ribs giving you some trouble, too? It looked like a piece of work climbing into the cab. Your hand hasn't left your side since you got in, either."

"Yeah, it hurts some."

With his free hand Dennis popped open the glove box and fished around until he felt what must have been the package of wipes. As he pulled it free, the back of his hand brushed against something hard. Peering in, he saw that it was a phone, face up in a thick protective case. His gut clenched a little at the odd incongruity, but he kept his mild concern to himself. Could have been a defunct phone, or maybe Akram had forgotten it was there. No big deal.

He closed the glove box and rubbed drying blood from his face and neck with some of the wipes, every movement coming with difficulty now. It didn't seem like the pain of a broken rib that kept his left hand at his side. It was more like a rib was poking at something deeper. Christ, how far were they from Seattle? Twenty minutes? Forty?

"Are you going to take the back roads all the way in? I think I'm in some trouble here."

Finishing up with the wipes, he balled them up and dropped them into a trashcan weighted down on the floor between driver and passenger with a sand-bag attachment at the bottom. Then he tossed the package into a recess on the dashboard.

"Back in the glove box, please," Akram said.

"What?"

"The wipes. Put them back in the glove box. Where you found them."

"You know, twenty years ago you wouldn't have been able to talk to me like that."

"You mean because you're white and I'm not." It wasn't a question.

"Basically. Plus, I'm a true American. You said yourself you're from Damascus." Dennis noticed the truck was accelerating. "Look, you're getting upset. Let's slow this rig down and act like adults. Once you drop me off at the medical center we'll never have to see each other again."

"Put the fucking wipes back where they belong!"

Time stretched until Dennis returned the wipes to the glove box, and then it stretched again as both men sat in strained silence. After several moments Dennis felt the truck settle to a more reasonable speed, and his breathing relaxed in turn.

"I apologize," Akram said. "It's just that I have certain standards of order."

"You've helped me out and I'm thankful for it." Dennis's mind turned back to the phone in the glove box. "But I don't need to be your problem. Why don't you let me out and I'll catch another ride."

"You wouldn't last an hour on your own. You'll find bottles of water under the seat."

It was the one thing that could have mollified Dennis in that instant. He reached down and retrieved a bottle. With some effort he unscrewed the lid, which was worth every pang once the water passed his lips and cascaded over his dry tongue and down his throat.

"So," Akram said, "are you one of these white nationalist types?"

Dennis gave a scoffing chuckle.

"I'm not afraid of the truth," Akram added.

"Yeah, I guess maybe I am. Does that offend you?"

"No. If anything it bores me. Racism is such a tired retreat."

"What about you? I assume you're a Muslim."

"Of course."

"Not exactly a religion of inclusiveness, is it?"

"What do you mean by that?"

"Well, your obsession with infidels. The way you oppress women and gays."

"How do *you* feel about women and gays, Dennis?"

"Oh fuck off. Don't go comparing yourself to me."

"Do you put faggots above Muslims?"

"I sure as hell don't want to stone them to death, or throw them off towers, or whatever you people do."

"But I suppose you'd be happy to bomb Muslims from the face of the earth."

"Terrorists, yeah."

"Ah, terrorism. Such a mystery to westerners. How else are poor Middle Eastern countries supposed to wage war against their powerful oppressors? They don't have navies and air forces."

The last thing Dennis wanted to waste his draining energies on was a political debate with a social justice warrior, so he let it drop. Both men fell into a kind of shared meditation. Dennis sensed that Akram didn't really want to pursue the matter any more than he did. In an effort to keep from giving voice to more angry thoughts, it was as if they silently agreed to content themselves with the lulling sound of tires humming across blacktop, their vision reduced to what was illuminated by the truck's merged cones of light, which guided them through the dark. Getting to Bay View Medical Center before Dennis lost consciousness, or worse, was the only goal that mattered.

He was nearly asleep when Akram mentioned a plan to connect with I-90, which would put them on a straight shot to the hospital. His head bobbed a few times and he was out.

❋ ❋ ❋

Dennis stands in the center of a windblown desert village. He is a boy, or made to feel like one. He is handed a gun, given rudimentary instructions on how to use it, and told to go practice with it until afternoon prayers. There will come a time when he will need every weapon at his disposal to fight back against the infidel oppressors of the West. "Who is my enemy?" he asks. "The whole world is your enemy," he is told. He takes several steps, then turns. The man who gave him the gun, and the answer to his question, is clad in desert attire and is walking away. "Father!" he calls out. The man turns around. Dennis lifts his weapon and takes aim. "Die like a dog, infidel!" The man waves his arms and opens his mouth wide to yell something back, but bullets rip through his chest and abdomen before he can utter a syllable. Each red hole seeps through the cotton fabric of his robe before he drops to the sand, lifeless and mute.

Someone is hollering in Arabic. Dennis hears the bark of rubber on pavement, but there's no pavement in the desert. Pain at his side. Did he shoot himself when he shot his father? Wait, his father wasn't an Arab. He didn't grow up in a desert. He was …

* * *

His eyes flashed open, his heart thumping as if two strong men were at it with alternating hammer blows. Still, the sound of Arabic at high volume. Something *like* Arabic anyway. Why did nothing look familiar through the windshield?

Slowly the world came back into focus. They had arrived in Seattle, and the city streets were a jarring contrast to the mountain roads they'd left behind. But they would have had to pass the trauma center to get to this part of downtown, wouldn't they?

He looked over at Akram, the source of the strange litany. The man's features were altered by anger the likes of which Dennis wasn't sure he'd ever seen before. Then he realized it wasn't anger. It was hatred that drew Akram's brow down between his deep-set eyes and pulled his cheeks taut across the bone beneath as he continued his high-pitched chanting.

They rounded onto a flat stretch of roadway, the financial district looming over them, but it was still difficult to make out their exact location. It didn't help that Dennis's vision dialed in and out of focus.

A flash of blue between buildings. Again. And again. Water. They were down by the piers. Alaskan Way.

The truth erupted like a flare in his brain. How could he have been so stupid? It was the third night of a summer music festival on one of the piers. His son had been talking about taking in some of the acts.

There would be hundreds of revelers milling about, even at this late hour.

The box truck accelerated and skidded into a turn, like a torpedo finding its trajectory. Akram's ululations intensified. Nearly tipping the truck onto its outside wheels, Akram gave the steering wheel one good crank and guided the vehicle—*weapon*—onto the pier. Dennis felt helpless to do anything more than observe.

A vague awareness of danger spread across the faces of those nearest the entrance to the pier. If he didn't do something to stop this, dozens might die by the time Akram reached the far edge of the platform. One of them could be his own son.

The first mass of people was less than twenty yards away. There was no way to avoid hitting all of them, unless—

He reached across the cab and clamped his hand over the horn. The sound it made was weaker than he'd hoped, and the pain at his side bloomed up into his chest and almost paralyzed him, but he didn't let go. With his other hand he forced the wheel, against Akram's considerable strength, and aimed for a gap between a hotdog vendor and the stage, which was awash in the flickering purples, blues, reds, and greens from the lighting rig. Dennis could hear music now, too. Bass and drums, bass and drums.

For a moment he thought he might actually pull this off without killing a soul, but he had wrenched the wheel as far off course as he was able, and it wasn't enough. The middle-aged man behind the hotdog stand was locked in place, staring with horror into the eyes of Death as it roared his way. He wanted to move. Dennis could see it in his bulging eyes. If the man had ever asked for death, he didn't want it now. But it wanted him. And it got him. There was no way he could have survived the tumult as they crashed into the stand and slammed it into the piling that also ended their progress.

Dennis was in a lot of pain, but he seemed to be intact. Akram was in worse shape. His head had struck the driver's-side window hard enough to spider-web it, and paint it red.

Good, Dennis thought. He hoped the sonofabitch would live long enough to wake up in agony, then croak regretting every fucking minute of his life.

A more pressing concern, however, was how to proceed without getting gunned down as a suspected terrorist himself. Already he could hear sirens swarming down the hill. Best to stay put, he figured, and do as they instruct once they arrive.

He only hoped they'd rush him to the hospital without asking a bunch of questions. Maybe he had the fortitude to tell his story once before fatigue and blood loss claimed him for the night, but not more than that. Better to inform the Bay View nurses, who might actually use some of the details to help keep him alive than a bunch of inquisitive cops who only wanted to clear the scene.

* * *

The smell was unmistakable. He knew where he was before he opened his eyes. It's not like he'd spent a lot of time in hospitals, but the masking, sterile odor hadn't change since he was a boy, hospitalized for complications stemming from an appendectomy. He'd smelled it again when his mother had been laid up after being mugged. The same chemical reek.

His mind grasped for reality, like hands on the rungs of a ladder. Why had the bastard bothered to pick him up? Had he wanted company? Not likely. Dennis figured it had more to do with peppering the game, adding a layer of complication to the investigation—and a layer of fear to the public's reception. But he knew that if you started trying to apply reason to the actions of madmen, you risked your own sanity in the process.

"Mr. Hobson?" It was a female voice, comforting.

He turned his head and saw the nurse who had rescued him from his own thoughts. Maybe twenty-five. No more than thirty. Akram's age. She wore her light brown hair neatly trimmed, and there wasn't a wrinkle to be seen on her spotless attire. Her smile was pleasant and credible.

"That's—" He coughed and took some water through a straw. "That's my name. Don't—" More coughing.

"Wear it out? I won't. There's someone who'd like to see you, if you're up for it."

"Cops?"

"No, they'll wait. But your son seems pretty anxious for a visit."

"Tony?" He pulled himself up a bit. "I'll be damned. Is he alone?"

"Yes, sir."

Sir, yet.

"Okay, send him in."

"Hey, Pop," Tony said, striding into the room. He was trying to play it like all of this was no big deal. Dennis had seen the walk and the attitude a thousand times before.

"How's it hangin', Toenail?"

The nurse smiled and left them alone.

"Like an anchor in the deep."

Dennis laughed until he coughed, then took another sip of water.

"I don't think you've ever given the same answer twice."

"I'm only sixteen. Give me time."

"Sixteen. Jesus, when did that happen? Yesterday you were hauling boogers out of your nose and wiping them on your pants. The ones you didn't eat, anyway."

Tony snickered a little.

"Hey, Pop, you really showed that snackbar the time of day, didn't you? They're calling you a hero. One down, couple billion to go. Ain't that right?"

"No, that ain't right. Why don't you come over here and have a seat, son."

Tony did as he was told.

"You think I did what I did because he was a Muslim? I stopped him because he was a killer."

"Ain't no difference. You said so yourself."

Dennis blanched because he knew it was true. He'd said that and worse.

"Listen, I got to know a little bit about our friend, Akram. At first I had him pegged as kind of a bigot. Then he started coming off like a goddamn SJW."

Tony laughed at that, glad to hear a little of his dad's old self.

"Well, the truth is, I could have lived with either of those. Not pleasant characteristics maybe, but not worth getting in a fist fight over, either. You see what I mean, son?"

"I guess I don't."

"I don't expect it to come to you all at once. Hell, I just about had to be knocked into tomorrow to get it through *my* thick skull. But I been feedin' you a lot of anger, boy. Anger at a lot of stuff it ain't worth being angry at. See, as long as Akram was just a Muslim truck driver willing to help me out of a tough spot, we were two men cut from different cloth, that's all. But as soon as I realized what he *really* was, I also realized what he wasn't. That make any sense?"

"Sonofabitch, Dad, I don't know."

"Look, I don't want you going through life hating and fearing everyone who's different from you. That sort of thinking just breeds more of the same. And just like the streets ain't filled with serial killers and rapists, they ain't overrun with terrorists, either. I know it's not a perfect comparison, but it's something for you to think on. Can you do that for me? Can you think on these things?"

"Yeah, I guess."

The boy was troubled by the change in his father. That was clear. But Dennis figured he'd come around. He wished he could take back about a thousand things he'd said over the years, but Tony was young and sharp. He'd see that there was more than one way to take in the world yet. If it could happen to a whipped old bugger like Dennis, it could sure as hell happen to his boy. Maybe it could happen to just about anyone.

He reached over and tousled his son's unruly mop of hair, but Tony pulled away.

"Got to go, Pop. Meetin' up with some friends."

Dennis watched Tony closely, trying to gauge his son's body language. Were his words sinking in as the boy stepped out of the room and left his father to his recovery, or were they breaking up against the wall Tony carried around with him and tumbling down to the floor unheeded?

Hard to say, as with just about everything else in life. And also like most things in life, only time would tell. Hopefully Tony would be listening when it did.

Dennis closed his eyes and did his best to get some sleep.

HOLY IS AS
HOLY DOES

He awoke knowing he was a different man than he had been the night before, that his life prior to this morning had been preamble. Today was a new beginning for Daniel Collier, and he breathed it in deeply.

Early morning light streamed in through his window, and he threw the threadbare curtains wide. He stood naked before the rising sun, which warmed his flesh through the glass.

There would be time enough for reverie at the top of the hill, so he quickly donned his rustic attire, fetched a light breakfast from the kitchen, and was out the door. He saddled up his steed, and as he rode off, the house felt large behind him, too much house for one man. But he vowed he would not be its only inhabitant for long. There was a wife in his future. Children, too. If one of those children turned out to be a boy, he would inherit an army of followers, because Daniel Collier intended to lead the pioneering people of America into a bright age of prosperity and greatness.

It would all begin on the hilltop.

Dandelions carpeted the crest of the hill, and he was tempted to lie down in their luxuriance, divest himself of his clothing and roll in them like an antediluvian god. Maybe later. He wasn't at the very top yet. A voice had been calling him there in his dreams, but it had taken him until now to work up the courage to make the climb. Now he was so convinced good news awaited him that he couldn't imagine why he'd put it off.

Tying his horse to a Russian olive tree, he made it the rest of the way on foot. From the rocky summit he could see to all corners of the prairie terrain. To the northeast, ranchland flourished. Cattle followed paths from one grazing pasture to another. In the west, fields of young wheat rolled like a wavering green blanket in the morning breeze. In the blink of an eye it would be autumn, and the healthy greens he saw before him would turn to brittle gold for the harvester's scythe.

The sky cracked open and Daniel fell to his knees in spontaneous prayer. He trained his gaze on a bright figure that floated down from the rent in the heavens. His dreams had not lied. Here came the Bringer of Truth, Angel of Light. Tears poured out of his eyes, and his hands shook as he held them in ready acceptance of his Savior's word.

The winged being halted in the air several yards above him, batting its wings to stay aloft. Its form was female perfection, naked yet chaste. The smile it wore showered grace down upon him. He knew that a lifetime of waiting was about to be recompensed as the angel opened its beautiful mouth and sang him his destiny.

* * *

"The path to righteousness is not a gilded path!" he shouted to the dozen or so members in attendance at the prayer meeting. "Nor is it lined with fine-smelling flowers. That path exists, if you haven't the stomach for the one true calling. Take, if you want, the beautiful and easy path that leads to an ocean of flames. I'll take the uneven, bramble-strewn way that leads me unto the glory of God!"

As the barn filled up with the exuberant praise of the worshippers gathered there, Daniel wondered what it would feel like to get a similar reaction from a crowd of fifty or more.

"We will meet with resistance along the path that has

been laid for us. Some will find our ways and customs odd, but there is no room for doubt that we are meant to rise to prominence among the competing denominations in this New World. Let those who oppose our subservience to the will of God tremble at the wisdom of His justice. Let them answer to Him for taking a stand against our piety!

"The good Lord has more in store for you and me than parrying the blows of the ignorant. He will watch over and protect us from the repercussions of men. We need only concern ourselves with the expansion of our church and our adherence to the will of the Almighty."

He dabbed at his forehead and neck with a handkerchief. All of the cheering congregants were men. That would have to change. Already he grew tired of the wind-battered faces of these farmers. Where were the bankers, and the bankers' daughters? He planned to exert certain ministerial claims over the women of this region, but they were infuriatingly slow to succumb to his charms.

He paused dramatically after the cheers of support died out.

"Go out into the world now and sing the new gospel. Enjoy your families in the coming nights. The church elders will have a mission for you soon. Great wealth wants to come into our church, but it is dependent on the absolute commitment of everyone present here today, and as many more as we can bring into the fold in a month's time."

The church elders consisted of exactly two members: Daniel and his faithful friend Theodore, who was seated in the barn with the other men, savoring every word that spilled from the minister's mouth. These were humble beginnings, but Daniel was convinced that an undertaking was only small if it was handled small. This new church of his would have to grow to meet his expectations and ambitions. *It* would rise to meet *him*. He wasn't about to shrink his ideals.

* * *

At Daniel's house, he and Theodore sat across from each other near a thriving fire, drinking from glasses of deep-red wine. Daniel had been considering banning wine, for purposes other than libation, but the timing wasn't right. With gold in the church coffers he would introduce an additional list of thou-shalt-nots, but for now he was happy to share a bottle with his friend.

"The letters pour in, Theodore. Even the newspapers are against us. So much resistance to the idea that a modern prophet could be handed an amendment to established scripture."

"They're the ones who will pay the price for their folly in the end," Theodore said in his serene but firm manner of speaking.

"In the end, yes, of course. If only I had more like you. Such confidence in the future!" Daniel said this with a histrionic clenching of his fist. "But we have yet to carve that future, Theodore. We must bend it to our will. A party of settlers will be passing through our county next week. I understand they'll be carrying gold. A lot of gold."

"Uh-huh," Theodore said.

"Paiute country, too. Sure would be a shame if those nice folks met up with a bunch of bloodthirsty savages."

"That *would* be a shame. And all for a little gold."

"For the good of the church, Theodore."

"Won't the survivors say it was us who massacred everyone? Or won't there be any survivors?"

"Come with me," Daniel said, exchanging his wine for a candle. He led Theodore to the back of the house, where a closed door stood at the end of a corridor. Choosing a key from a large ring, he unlocked the door.

The two men entered a small, windowless room. Everything in range of the candlelight was covered with white sheets. Furniture, crates ... Daniel couldn't even remember everything that was still waiting here to be unpacked since his arrival out west. He crossed directly to the tallest item in the room and smiled at Theodore.

"What do you suppose this is?" he asked.

"I'm sure I have no idea."

"Remove the sheet."

Theodore reached hesitantly for the covering, as if pulling it away might reveal a caged animal. Once it was pulled aside he exhaled loudly in relief. "Why, it's a wardrobe."

"Precisely. A wardrobe. But not just any wardrobe. This wardrobe is special."

"What do you mean, special?"

"Look inside." He knew Theodore would go to the ends of the earth for him, but it was good to reinforce the man's allegiance from time to time.

With a glance at Daniel, Theodore stepped to the wardrobe and threw open its doors. Daniel purposely kept the light of his candle from revealing the contents of the tall wooden closet, but the dense odor of aged leather wafted out immediately. Finally he tilted his candlestick so that it illuminated the interior.

Theodore took a step back and looked at Daniel. "I don't understand. This is Indian dress, is it not?"

Daniel smiled and nodded. "Easier to make our own Indians than convince real ones to join our cause, yes?"

"Where did you get these?"

"I've been collecting them. You aren't going cold on me, are you?"

"No, it's just—"

"Good, I wouldn't want to have to make public certain indiscretions from your past."

"There'll be no need for that. I'll organize the ambush straightaway."

"I knew I could count on you, Theodore. I am blessed to have you at my side."

Theodore gave a perfunctory nod as Daniel shut the wardrobe.

"Our wine has had sufficient time to breathe, I should

think," Daniel led his underling into the corridor and locked up the room before returning to the fire.

* * *

Standing atop a bluff overlooking the site that was about to go down in history—the good Lord willing—Daniel Collier had doubts. Not about the nature of his plan or the justification for it, but doubts about whether or not his men could be relied on to carry out their orders. They all seemed to be behind him in this, but he knew that when the wagon train was stopped, and women and children began spilling onto the road to see what was going on, his men would have second thoughts.

He ducked behind a nearby cottonwood and sat down with his back against the knotty trunk. The smell of prairie grass, slightly sharp, was strong, and he took to winding blades of it around his index fingers before yanking them from the ground. A small group of men huddled nearby, and Daniel could see how ridiculous the disguises looked. It was one thing to have the appropriate attire, quite another to know how to fit it properly. They would fool some of the settlers, but others would see right through them. He had thought it would be a good idea to leave some survivors behind, to spread the word of what was about to happen. The incident would grow in scope with each retelling, which might keep outsiders from moving into the area in droves. But maybe they *would* have to kill them all, as Theodore had suggested. His church wasn't yet strong enough to shoulder the blame for something of this magnitude.

The rattling grind of wagon wheels on dry earth came with shocking suddenness. At the first sound of the settlers' approach he was up like a shot, crouching as he went from man to man and issued the command to take up battle positions. He knew it would be no battle. It would be a slaughter, a decimation. But it could do his men's fighting spirit no harm to have them think this wagon train was a threat to their personal safety. That's how he'd sold it, and that's how they'd bought it. Stolen gold it was in those wagons, according to his story. And each and every member of the Blackert party was as cold blooded as they came. Only he and Theodore knew that the Blackerts and their associates had come upon their gold through the sale of prime land farther east. They'd simply pooled their income, joined forces, and pulled up stakes in search of warmer climes.

Daniel and his men set themselves up along the edge of trees that gave way to a steep drop leading down into the meadow the Blackert party would soon be passing through. Theodore and his contingent manned a ridge opposite, armed with bows and tomahawks for the sake of realism. Everyone had a rifle slung at their side for good measure.

The settlers came snaking into the meadow presently, trailing great plumes of dust. It was a holy vision, almost as holy as the angel who had visited Daniel on the hilltop all those months ago. He yearned for the means to preserve the next hour for eternity. The Bible itself contained no scene more memorable than what was about to unfold on these plains before his very eyes.

He let out a holler, which passed among the men until it reached Adam Jacoby, Lance Hartly, and Jules Warren, the party assigned to stopping the wagons. Daniel watched with wide, hopeful eyes as the men thundered down the hillside on horseback, whooping in their best imitation of a Paiute war cry and swinging tomahawks above their heads. Daniel let out a second holler, this one signaling the remaining men to descend upon the rest of the stalled wagon train. Their descent was a visual signal to the men on Theodore's side to do likewise.

It was at a leisurely pace that Daniel navigated the slope down to the meadow. He had no interest in partaking of the violence, but he wanted to bear witness. His horror mounted, however, as he neared the scene on foot. There was no beauty here, nothing sublime. The screams of women and children being dragged from the backs of wagons by their hair filled his ears.

The men folk were quickly dispatched with rifles, but women were cruelly slain in front of their children. Young girls were stripped naked and beaten to death. Boys were forced to take it all in before meeting with similar fates.

Daniel circled the mayhem in disbelief, as if he were Dante being led through a ditch of hell by an unseen Virgil. What kind of monsters had he created? It wasn't supposed to feel this way. Here was Lance, tearing chunks out of a woman's neck with a hunting knife. There was Jules, tying a boy no more than twelve to a wagon wheel by the neck and striking the flank of the horse at the front of the wagon. The horse whickered and fled, and the boy's throat took the full weight of the wagon at each rotation of the wheel. Daniel clearly heard the boy's broken screams, but he probably only imagined the *blump, blump* of his head smacking the uneven earth as the wagon charted an erratic course across the meadow.

He spotted Theodore in the madness and went to him.

"Theodore, what goes on? They carry this thing too far." He laid a trembling hand on his friend's shoulder.

Theodore's eyes were dead coals. "Do not ever speak to me of this day," he said.

To Daniel's dismay, the man returned to the fray and began clubbing children to death with the blunt end of his tomahawk.

"*Theodore!*" he screamed, but his friend was lost in a hurricane of bloodlust.

Disgust rose up in Daniel, and he turned away from the bloodshed he'd called for. His great religious moment felt more like a badge of shame as he wound his way back into the hills toward home, terrified and alone

* * *

Theodore would come to him. Sooner or later his trustworthy companion would deliver a report of the afternoon's proceedings. *Someone* would come to him. They couldn't leave him to suffer his burden and puzzle out the next steps by himself.

But it grew dark all around, and still no one came to put his mind at ease. Did they not understand how keenly he felt the impact of the day's events? Did they not appreciate the responsibility he shouldered?

"*Come to me!*" He flung his empty whiskey glass into the fireplace, where it exploded with a loud report. Then he fell into his chair.

A knock at the back door. A single knock.

"Well, it's about time." He dragged himself out of the chair and stumbled his way to the back of the house. "Been a long time since you've been good and drunk, Daniel," he slurred to himself and laughed. "Can't hold your liquor."

He released the latch, but the door wouldn't budge. Looking up he remembered bolting it. He'd be bolting his doors from now on, he had a feeling.

"That you, Theodore?" He fumbled with the wooden bolt. "Good idea, coming to the back door. Can't be too careful."

Another solitary knock, followed by silence.

Finally the bolt slipped out of its notch and Daniel was able to open the door. At first all he saw were the boughs of a couple of old oak trees in the distance, cradling the crescent moon as a cool evening breeze blew through them. But when he looked down, his eyes met the stolid faces of two small children, a boy and a girl.

"This is one of my faces," the boy said, "but I have another one."

"Wha—"

Whatever Daniel meant to say was cut short by horrified disbelief as he watched the boy reach up to his own forehead with both hands and peel the skin of his face downward until it hung from his chin in a loose, gory flap.

"You did this to me." The boy's voice was wetter now. He turned his head toward the girl, as if giving her a cue.

"Do you want to see what you did to me?" she asked, too sweetly.

Daniel shook his head but no words would come.

The girl looked over at the boy. "He doesn't want to see." She gave an exaggerated pout and looked back up at Daniel. "But he's going to." Something dark had come into her voice, and she set about undoing the middle buttons of her dress, which he noticed was bloodstained. A bullet had ripped through the center of her little body, apparently, leaving behind the hideous wound she now flaunted.

"You have changed us," the children said in unison. "Now it's our turn to change you."

He tried to slam the door on them, but they were too quick. They shot around him and ran upstairs, giggling all the way. Daniel teetered for a moment as fear squeezed out the dregs of his inebriation. When he finally managed to shut the door—and refasten the bolt—it was on sober but wobbly legs that he gazed at the foot of the stairs.

"I'll teach you to cut my face off with your Indian axe!" The boy's voice could have been coming from any of the upstairs rooms.

"Shoot *me* in the tummy, will you?" the girl's voice charged. "We'll see about that."

"You've got the wrong man," Daniel said, mounting the stairs. "I swear I didn't touch either of you. I harmed no one!"

The children giggled some more.

Don't go up there, a voice in the back of his mind cautioned. But he knew he had to. What else could he do, run? Flee from his own house? Never. If only his guiding angel would come to him now, tell him what to do, the way she had told him of his destiny. How later, in his dreams, she had wiped away his doubts and shown him the wisdom of murdering the Blackert party.

But wait, that hadn't turned out to be so wise. He was confused. Why had the angel misled him?

The last step groaned under his weight and brought him out of his thoughts, back to his predicament.

"Okay, children. Where are you?" He tried to sound calm but didn't. "Come on out, and let's talk this through." He contemplated going back for the candle but decided it wouldn't be of any real use. The feeble moonlight would suffice. That and the flickering firelight from below.

"You're a bad, bad man." It was both voices together again, but he still couldn't tell which room they were in.

Two rows of doors ran parallel to the staircase. He had hoped at least one of these rooms would be home to a child one day. How had he lost sight of that simple wish?

He stepped to the first door on the left side of the stairs. It popped free of its latch with ease when he turned the ceramic knob, and he steeled himself for a lunge into the darkness beyond.

But something caught his attention at the far end of the hall. Where moonlight stole in through a grimy window, he could make out the dead-still outlines of the two children. His blood seemed to drain away at the sight of them, so smug in their accusatory stance, their fearless communion with the dark. He envied them that, and he hated them for seeing more than he saw, for knowing more than he knew.

"*Wretched spawn!*" he shrieked.

As he ran full speed down the length of the hall, he could see the silhouettes of their heads turn to look at each other, and again they giggled. Their laughter crescendoed and echoed in his brain, but he would soon put a stop to that!

He leaped into the air, wanting to pounce on the little brats, but they had vanished beneath him and he had overshot his mark. The window shattered in a spray of broken glass as he sailed through the casement, awash in moonlight. An instant before he collided with the ground, the moon flashed him the smile of a welcoming angel.

BARBICIDE

"**I**'m ready for you, Jim," Charles said, sweeping a lush pile of light brown hair into a dustpan. "Why don't you have a seat right over here." He tapped the back of a jet-black barber's chair.

Jim eyed the overweight man who had been his barber for almost twenty years over the top of his *Sports Illustrated*. Charles Dyer hadn't dropped or gained a pound in all that time, it seemed. Still the same eggplant of a man he'd always been, just a little grayer at the sideburns, maybe sporting a few more wrinkles. Wasn't as quick to smile. *It happens to the best of us*, Jim mused, setting the magazine aside and stepping behind the register to the chair that Charles had indicated.

"What are we doing today," Charles wanted to know as he stared patiently at Jim in the mirror. It was a casual formality, the answer always being the same.

"Why don't we take an inch off the back. Maybe clip the sides and trim the top."

Charles nodded, unfurled a purple cape and gingerly fastened it around Jim's neck. Soon the mundane business of a routine haircut was underway.

Barbicide, the glass jar on Charles's work station read. Sitting in the cylinder filled with blue disinfectant were shears and a comb. Jim thought it was the kind of tube you might expect to see a deformed fetus floating in, staring out at you with the one unblinking eye left in its little head.

He didn't have much of a plan. He'd locked the door once

he was inside and ascertained that he was the only customer in the place. Some kind of extortion, he figured. Just enough to make Charles squirm. It would be satisfying to have something to hold over the bastard's head. That was as far as he intended to take things.

But now the Barbicide was on his mind.

"You been busy?" he asked.

"Oh, you know. Feast or famine. Kind of quiet today, but yesterday I had to beat 'em out the door with a stick."

"How's Julie?" Jim watched in the mirror, but Charles kept his gaze averted.

"She's fine." A pause. "Rachel?"

"Fine," Jim replied.

Snip, snip.

"She's a hell of a fuck when she wants to be. Isn't that right, Charles?"

The shears slipped from Charles's hand and hit the floor. Now he stared directly into Jim's eyes in the mirror.

"What the hell are you talking about?"

"You really ought to watch that habit of yours."

"What habit?"

"Dropping things. Like monogrammed handkerchiefs. It took me about thirty seconds to realize it belonged to you. Are you going to deny it?"

"Deny what? You don't think—"

"Oh, spare me the bullshit. I've been coming here long enough to see you blow your nose a time or two. I know that monogrammed handkerchiefs are about the only luxury you allow yourself."

Charles slowly turned Jim's chair so he could face him.

"Have you confronted Rachel?"

"No."

"Why not?"

"I thought maybe you and I could come to an agreement."

"Are you trying to blackmail me? Jesus, Jim. You know I don't have a pot to piss in."

Jim shrugged and peeled the cape away from his neck as he stood.

"That's true. Maybe it's not the best way to proceed here."

Now the barber was nervous. It was in his eyes, a primal emotion. It felt good to be the cause of such a thing. Better than Jim would have imagined. He reached for the jar of Barbicide.

"What the ..." Charles trailed off, as if he had his answer before he could get the question all the way out.

"Drink it," Jim commanded.

"You're out of your mind."

"*Drink it!*" He set the Barbicide down closer to Charles and went to the desk phone by the register. "Or should I give Julie a call?"

"What kind of Hobson's choice is that? Either you expose me to my wife or I die horribly from toxicity?"

"You won't die, Charles. Christ, I've done a little research. You'll get sick. You'll have the shits for a day or so. But you'll be fine. I just want you to know that I won't be toyed with. Your affair with Rachel is over."

"I'll never see her again, I swear!"

"Drink the fucking disinfectant. Then I'll believe you, and you'll know that I mean business."

Charles didn't bother arguing further. He eyed the Barbicide for a moment, then reached for it and quickly removed the sterilized implements. Throwing Jim one last pleading look, and catching only a glare of stony anticipation, he guzzled as much of the Barbicide as he could before his body refused to take any more.

Jim watched him gurgle and cough. Charles's fingers let go of the jar, which shattered when it hit the floor.

"Clumsy," Jim said, shaking his head.

Charles went down on one knee. "It ... burns." His hands went to his throat and he began to tremble. Sweat broke out on his forehead, then his arms. The shakes worsened and he fell over onto his side. Breath came in shallow gasps as he fought for his life. A trickle of blood ran from one nostril.

"You said ... it ... wouldn't ..."

"I lied. For all I know you'll be dead in minutes. Dear God, suicide is one thing, but to do it in front of me. What were you trying to convey? I suppose we'll never know for sure, but maybe it was your way of atoning for what you did. Rachel will of course come clean about everything as soon as she finds out about this."

Charles stared at him, his eyes wide with terror, and then he was gone.

Jim fished his phone out of a pocket and dialed 911 as he unlocked the door and stepped outside, hoping there was a brilliant actor somewhere deep inside him. He was about to need his help.

THE TREE MUMBLERS

Overnight, strange figures began appearing throughout Seattle. Tree mumblers, we started calling them, because each one stood several feet away from a tree, facing the trunk and muttering quietly at it. No one was quite sure which held sway, the trees or the mumblers. All anyone knew for certain was that it was damned odd. Even the six o'clock news teams couldn't decide if the story should be played for laughs, screams, or scientific interest. Imagine, a scoop too bizarre for television news to pitch across the home plate of middle America.

I saw my first tree mumbler on the university campus, on my way from the ladies' room in Denham Hall to the north parking garage. I'd passed a student with an armful of tattoos, which got me thinking how I used to secretly scoff at such people. What if they grew to regret them? But I was starting to see that concentrating on post-modern American literature as a grad student had been a lot like getting a tattoo. Here I was, a lecturer on Barth and Pynchon who could no longer stomach the work of either writer. Now I spent my summers steeped in the luxurious prose of the Victorians, but the metafictional die had been cast. There was no turning back.

What was really on my mind was a yearning to take the longest bath of my life as soon as I got home. That's when I spotted the hooded figure facing an elm tree with closed eyes, as if hypnotized or awaiting instruction, all the while mumbling under his breath. He was off the pavement, standing barefoot in the grass. There was something disquieting about him. Disquieting and intriguing. I took a seat on a nearby bench.

There was nothing unusual about seeing a druid behaving strangely in Seattle. That's what I called them, anyway. Young kids wearing hoodies that sported patches for bands like Lamb of God, Mastadon, and Rammstein. Some were homeless. Others tagged along and pretended to be. Like I say, the type wasn't unusual. But this tree mumbler was something else entirely. Though his lips moved ceaselessly, his eyes stayed closed. Wet or greasy strands of hair jutted from the sides of his hood. His skin looked unhealthy. Even the fingertips that poked out of his fingerless gloves were pallid.

Then, without warning, he rotated his head in my direction. His eyelids flashed open, revealing not eyes, but orbs of blue luminescence. The blue light seemed to envelop me, but it also entered me—and not just through my eyes. It poured into my ears, nose, and mouth, filling voids I didn't know I possessed. The light gave me vigor and focus. I was becoming ... one of them.

I've always loved cherry trees, so that's the type of tree I chose. It doesn't really matter what you pick, though, since your eyes remain closed most of the time. We're told in the beginning that we're waiting for a revelation, that when we're strong enough in number, the trees will share a great secret with us.

Until then, we mumble.

I recently overheard a talkative old lady comment to her friend that I may be the first woman mumbler. I don't think gender is going to play a role in the coming age, though.

A few moments ago, I stole a glance to my right because I heard the rustling of paper. A young man sits cross-legged on the grass nearby, feverishly jotting down notes of some kind. For the life of me I can't guess what he feels so compelled to write about.

A POUND OF FLESH

Brenda was forty-five minutes late, which gave Desmond an excuse to take one more lap through the rooms of his apartment. Everything had to be right. She'd forgiven him and agreed to an evening of dinner, wine, and ... Well, she hadn't exactly agreed to the last part yet, but he was hopeful. He had an expensive bottle of her favorite Sangiovese on hand and a kettle of homemade spaghetti sauce bubbling on the stove, so all he had to do was convince her to stay in and watch movies instead of going out after dinner. The rest would be a cinch. But the apartment had to be perfect.

His stint in the military probably didn't help his obsessive – compulsive outlook on cleanliness. Nor did his closeness to God, Whose own insistence on neatness was well documented. But Desmond didn't give a shit. He loved God and kept his lodgings clean—didn't see a thing wrong with either position and was happy to exchange words with anyone who did.

Bedroom: drum-tight bedclothes, not a stitch of clothing on the floor, air mildly scented—great. Office: she probably wouldn't go in there, but if she did she'd find a meticulously organized computer station—super. Living room: spotless; enough throw pillows on the couch to necessitate close seating, nothing but a bowl of nuts on the glass-topped coffee table—excellent. Kitchen: blindingly spick-and-span, the air a rich stew of garlic and tomato—right on. He was ready. Now, if Brenda would only show up before his nervousness turned to anger.

The intercom buzzer sounded. His body relaxed, which

made him realize how keyed up he'd allowed himself to get.

He pressed talk. "That you, Brenda?" There was still more than a little leftover Persian Gulf paranoia in his blood.

"Mr. Sachs?" A man's voice.

Desmond's fingers quivered as they toggled the talk/listen button. "Who is this?"

"Name's Comstock. Walter Comstock. Just need a second of your time."

Desmond waited for the stranger to explain himself, but there was only silence.

"Look, I'm expecting company. Why don't you beat down someone else's door?"

"Won't take but a minute, Mr. Sachs. I have a legal matter to discuss with you."

"It's almost seven-thirty in the goddamn evening."

"It involves a rather large sum of money."

That got Desmond's attention. Maybe the man was worth listening to after all. If there was one thing Desmond Sachs felt almost as strongly about as the Bread of Life, it was the importance of a fluid economy.

He buzzed the man into the building and considered leaving the door ajar for him but in the end decided to make him knock. After one quick series of staccato raps, Desmond opened the door wide. Before him stood a man as short as it was possible to get without being a proper dwarf. He was decked out in a double-breasted, pin-striped suit and topped with a fedora. Might have been in his early fifties. He wore gloves and held a briefcase at his side.

"Good evening, Mr. Sachs," the man said with a tug of his hat brim. His voice was mellow and calming.

Desmond stepped aside and gestured for Walter Comstock to enter, which he did, making himself at home by placing the briefcase on the coffee table and climbing onto the sofa.

"What's this all about? I'm in a bit of a hurry." Desmond shut the door and crossed his arms.

Walter Comstock smiled, one arm on a hill of throw pillows. "You're a military man. Army. Did a three-year tour that included the Iraq War."

"Listen, I—"

"You've dished up some large talk about your honorable discharge from service, but I have to say, Mr. Sachs, that my research failed to turn up anything on your military record more complimentary than the time you beat up a boy in Fallujah for refusing to try a chocolate bar."

"You bug-eyed little ... Who do you think you are, anyway? I ought to dwarf-toss your ass right out that fucking window."

"Yes, your knack for colorful insults comes up several times, as I recall. Had quite a time with the ladies, too, didn't you? Seems that you left more than a few village damsels in quite a state. I appreciate that spreading democracy is tiring work, but my, my."

Desmond took a seat in a chair near one end of the sofa and stared darkly at the little man with the great big nerve. He spoke through gritted teeth. "You said something about money. I suggest you cut to the chase and get out of my life before my dinner guest arrives."

"Oh, we've got plenty of time. Smells delicious, by the way. Italian?"

"What do you want with me? What's in the briefcase?"

"Your generation is so impatient. No zest for pacing. Everything's got to be done on the go, all of a sudden." Comstock snapped his fingers frantically as he delivered this. "True, I'm here on business, but there's no reason we can't get to know each other a bit first. I like to know who I'm dealing with." His look and tone had cooled several degrees.

Desmond didn't like to admit it, but he was thrown off guard by the diminutive man. He knew that if the evening turned violent, scrapping with a man the size of Comstock would be awkward. He didn't like it. It narrowed his options.

"I'd better check the sauce," Desmond said.

He walked briskly to the kitchen and exhaled, his face

blocked from Comstock's view by a row of cupboards above a bar-style countertop. He stirred the pot of sauce with a wooden spoon, knowing the man in the other room would be able to see that much, but his face was tight with hatred toward the intrusive little bastard. He needed a plan, and he needed to calm down.

The oven clock showed seven-twenty-seven. Where the fuck was Brenda? Not that he wanted her and Walter Comstock in his apartment at the same time, especially considering what the man seemed to know of his past, but maybe her arrival would convince the obstinate prick to leave.

"Mr. Sachs," Walter Comstock called from the other room, "what do you suppose is keeping your dinner date?"

Something about the way he said it set off an alarm that echoed in Desmond's brain. Had the fucker done something to Brenda? God help him if he had. That was Desmond's job, and he was territorial about it, Comstock's size be damned.

"Should be here any minute." He struggled to keep his cool.

"You've stopped stirring. Something eating you?"

"Okay, you little shit!" Desmond rushed back into the living room and pointed a finger at his uninvited guest. "If you've got something to say, say it. Otherwise, there's the door." He aimed his pointing finger in that direction. His chest heaved with deep, rapid breaths.

Any pretense of amusement fell away from Walter Comstock's expression. He was all business as he pushed himself to the edge of the sofa, his toes barely sweeping the floor, and leaned forward to pop the thumb-operated clasps of the briefcase. It opened maybe a quarter of an inch, and he seemed happy to leave it at that for the time being.

Avarice flushed out some of Desmond's anger as soon as he heard the *plick-plick* of the clasps. His mouth watered and he sat back down.

"Brenda Nottingham is not a woman of means, Mr. Sachs."

Okay, so he knew her. That didn't mean he'd done anything to her. *Hear the man out.*

"But her father is. He hires me for odd jobs. P. I. work, research, that sort of thing. He was less than pleased when his daughter told him she'd been worked over by a disgruntled boy-friend."

"Now wait a minute. What are you suggesting?"

"Come now, Mr. Sachs. I've seen her medical file. She was beaten until her face was a bloody mass, and she swears you're the puke who did it. That's good enough for Mr. Nottingham, and it's good enough for me."

"That lying bitch! She said she wanted to make up. That's what tonight was all about. Fuck if I haven't been had. So you're here to pay me off, I suppose. Just enough lettuce to send me packing without any complaint. Is that it?"

"I'm afraid it isn't quite that simple. We don't care where you choose to live. You can move in next door to Brenda for all I care. Our eyes are on you now. That isn't likely to change."

"Then what's in the briefcase? Let's have it."

"Why don't you see for yourself." He rotated it in Desmond's direction.

Desmond eased it all the way open and his enthusiasm quickly faded. Empty, except for some kind of plastic lining affixed to the interior with masking tape.

"Nothing? What the fuck? You said this was about money."

"That was a white lie, I'm afraid, to get you to let me in."

"You've got some nerve, little man. And now that you're in, what's the plan?"

Comstock's face brightened some. "I'm afraid you aren't going to like this part very much."

He jumped the short distance off the couch and swiftly reached inside his blazer with a gloved hand. Every bit as swiftly, his hand came out again, brandishing a coil of fine wire cable with shiny metal rings attached at either end. Desmond had never seen a diamond-wire saw before, but he knew that's what he was looking at. He had no time to react. Walter

Comstock was on him in a leap, wrapping the wire around Desmond's left wrist and drawing it back and forth, index fingers hooked like claws through the rings. The men toppled over in Desmond's chair, but Comstock was attached like a wood tick, his little legs wrapped tightly around one of Desmond's. Desmond screamed and flailed, trying desperately to find Comstock with one of his aimless swings, but his efforts had no effect on the deadly precision of the small man's task.

Soon—but not soon enough—it was over. Comstock stood and dangled the prize of Desmond's left hand in front of its previous owner's face by the little finger.

"Your dues have been paid, Mr. Sachs," he said, barely out of breath. "No need to get up. I'll see myself out." He dropped the bloody hand, and the saw, into the briefcase, snapped it closed, and removed it from the coffee table. "You won't want to say anything truthful about this to anyone. You may not believe it now, but there are worse things that can be done to you, and I'm adept at all of them."

He closed the door quietly behind him and left Desmond to the pain and mess of what had passed between them.

Desmond didn't know how he'd deal with Mr. Nottingham and his little rat-man lackey, but there was time for decisions of that magnitude. First things first. He crawled to the kitchen, climbed to his feet with the help of the oven, and pushed the pot of spaghetti sauce to the back of the stove. Sauce spilled over the edge and smoked where it hit the hot burner. He held his bleeding stump before him, closed his eyes, and gritted his teeth. Then, as if stamping out a cockroach, he slammed the oozing end of his left arm directly onto the red-hot element and held it there.

A scream like nothing he'd ever heard issued from his mouth and rattled the dishware above the stovetop, and a lingering moment later, Desmond Sachs collapsed to the floor in a swoon.

DAY OF RAGE

Blake awoke to the cool dampness of nightmare sweat on the bedsheet, breathing heavily with the knowledge that something had pursued him through fens and hollows while his eyes had darted back and forth behind closed lids. He kicked off the covers in anger, then flung his legs over the edge of the bed to sit and stew. Finally he stomped to the kitchen and downed two tall glasses of tap water in quick succession. Even his swallows were angry.

Halfway through a breakfast of instant oatmeal and grapefruit juice, he began thinking about free will, a favorite debate item from his college days. He stood staunchly on the side of the determinists, unable to comprehend the true nature of choice. What was it if not an uncaused event, since we can't be held accountable for a *caused* event? His brain simply could not make choice plausible. As far as he was concerned, if one event was caused, then all events were caused.

He could trace his philosophical curiosity to a single childhood incident. A neighborhood bully had been pulling him too fast in a Radio Flyer wagon, and when one of the front wheels struck the edge of an uplifted section of sidewalk, he'd tumbled into the street and scraped his palms bloody. He hadn't cried, only stared at his raw hands, thinking that surely if he'd woken up thirty seconds earlier that morning he never would have fallen out of the wagon. Might never have crawled into it to begin with.

Despite his interest in the free-will debate, Blake had

never set out to prove he was right. The day of rage he'd awoken into was the perfect goad.

His experiments started out small. He rented a Buick, despite owning a perfectly good Hyundai, and drove almost fifty miles to have lunch in a small town he'd never been to before. He was surprised to make it that far with his trials, but it proved nothing. Surely he'd come up against a wall soon, over which no amount of so-called choice could catapult him.

Dinner would be Chinese, he decided. He hated Chinese. Loathed every morsel he'd ever tasted. But there he sat at the Five Star Dragon's smallest table, in its darkest corner, full to bursting with sweet-and-sour shrimp, egg rolls, and green tea.

"Your fortune cookie, sir," the overly polite waiter said, presenting the most boring of all desserts on a small plate with the check.

Movement out the window caught his eye. A homeless man was picking his nose and peering into a refuse bin. Anger surged through the veins of Blake's neck, up into his temples and forehead. Who did this guy think he was that he could just stand around on a public sidewalk, picking his nose while people were trying to eat inside?

His fist came down inadvertently on the fortune cookie. The noise of the plate as it clattered in little circles startled a family in a nearby booth. It also fueled his rage. Tearing his gaze from the man outside, he noticed something odd. There was no fortune amid the cookie rubble before him. His fate was in his own hands, it appeared.

"What do I care?" he shouted, to the chagrin of everyone in the restaurant.

He tossed a couple of bills on the table and made for the front door.

"Asshole," he heard someone say as he pushed open the door.

"Go fuck yourself," he called back over his shoulder.

And then he was outside with the bum. He studied him for a moment in the violet-tinged twilight before making his presence known.

"Hey! You got a fuckin' problem?"

The man, older than Blake had figured from inside, stood to full height and turned to face his questioner. He was gaunt and wizened. Used up. Worthless.

"I asked you a goddamn question. You deaf?"

"Don't want no trouble. Just looking for something to eat ..." The voice was low and guttural, the obvious by-product of years of excessive drinking.

"Oh, you're hungry! I'm sorry, I didn't realize. Here, why don't you have some Chinese."

He stepped up to the man and pushed two fingers deep down inside his own throat. His gag reflex came on quickly. Two fruitless retches. Three. Then gold. Up came dinner in a veritable Yangtze of noodles, egg, shrimp, and tea. All of it sprayed onto the homeless man with the sound of a paper bag being wadded up.

"I didn't do nothin' to you," the man said, maddeningly unfazed, except for the slow, incredulous shaking of his head.

A black Cadillac Escalade barreled through the nearest intersection.

"No? Well I'm sure as shit going to do something to you."

He cocked both arms and launched his open palms into the stranger's chest, heaving him off the curb and into the path of the onrushing Cadillac.

"Don't!" the man yelled, but he was powerless to stop the work of gravity and inertia. Only the passenger-side mirror made contact, but it was the man's head that took the force of the blow, and the vehicle was moving so fast. A crimson gout flared from the bum's temple as he whirled around and slammed into a parked car before slumping to the pavement. The Cadillac didn't even slow.

Blake took the scene in for a moment before walking away in a daze, knowing that if the man wasn't already dead he soon would be. He'd never killed anything more significant than a spider. He was a quick study, apparently.

Walking turned to running as he headed down Jefferson Way, which would lead him to the highest bridge in town. His day of rage was nearly over.

Was it free will or was it causation that had pointed his feet toward the bridge? He couldn't decide for sure, but he stayed on course to the bitter end.

THE WORST IS
YET TO COME

L yndon knew he wasn't supposed to play on Duff Kendrick's farm, but it was impossible to resist. Rusting scraps of ancient farming equipment littered the yard. Railroad ties lay strewn in an adjacent pasture, sad reminders of corrals that were never built, cattle chutes left in need of mending. Sagebrush and leafy spurge ran riot among it all, right up to the front door of the ramshackle house. Everything about the place was paradise to a boy like Lyndon.

Or would have been, if not for the rumors. Area boys were disappearing in Bradley County, and there weren't a lot of clues. But kids were good at filling in gaps, and it didn't take long for the collective finger of Lyndon's circle of friends to point to Duff Kendrick—Duffer, as he was commonly called—as a prime suspect.

He approached cautiously from the field behind the Kendrick farm. The sun melted like topping on the horizon, which was the best time to strike. Well, maybe not strike ... forage. Lyndon wasn't a junk expert, but he knew what he liked, and Duffer Kendrick's dilapidated farm was a gold mine. These expeditions also gave Lyndon an opportunity to do a little spying.

As he followed his usual course through high weeds and fossils of the Industrial Age, Lyndon's eyes fell on something that hadn't been there during his last scavenging run. Some kind of black metal cabinet off to the right, in a particularly shabby part of the yard. It was a safe, he realized as he drew near. Its door hung wide open, like an inviting amusement—or a hungry mouth, he tried to warn himself. He rested one hand on top, the other on the door. It was big enough for him to get into, and he was already wondering how he might get it home and convert it into a bunker or hiding place.

His father had cautioned him against playing in things that could trap him, like ancient refrigerators. When the old man had been drinking, such cautionary tales were often punctuated with a backhand across the face or a kick to the shin. But this was different. The door of the large black safe was heavy, and the way the whole thing was canted backward in a shallow cleft of soil, he didn't see how the door could possibly close on him. Besides, it probably wouldn't lock even if it did shut. All he wanted was to peek at the world from inside the thing, try it on for size.

As he stepped inside, it became clear that there was more to his curiosity than wanting an unusual perspective on Duffer's farm. Still facing the back wall of the safe, Lyndon felt the low tingle of a delicious fear. Not only was he doing something Father would have objected to in the harshest terms—would have belt-whipped him for—but it was something not every boy would have had the nerve to do. Finally he turned around and felt as though he'd conquered something. Duffer's yard, framed by the doorway of the safe, seemed small, and Lyndon wondered if the whole world would seem a little smaller from now on.

But before he could step out of the safe to find out, it began to tip backward. He struggled for the opening but was thrown off balance by the movement. The safe collided hard with the earth, and all motion ceased, except for the door, which seemed to swing inward in slow motion. He reached up, hoping to block it, keep it from latching shut … but he wasn't quick enough. A moment later he was in the most complete, suffocating darkness he had ever known.

His own breathing deafened him to other sounds, if there

were any. Instinct urged him to try the door, but fear—no longer delicious—kept him motionless, except for the rapid, heavy breaths he drew. He wondered how much air he had in the small space, and his breathing quickened at the thought.

Slowly, his right hand moved in the darkness, seeking the cool steel of the door above him. He pressed his palm flat against the surface, then brought up his other hand. With both hands in position he began to push. For a tiny piece of an instant he thought the door might relent, but it was only an illusion caused by the slight give of his wrists and the fleshiest parts of his palms. The latch was secured. Escape was hopeless.

Mrs. Finch, his sixth-grade teacher, had told the class once that it was important never to panic in an emergency, that it only made matters worse. But caught up in the worst emergency of his life, Lyndon was surprised to feel more terrified of trying to remain calm than he was of throwing a useless fit. He'd rather make noise and tire himself out than cross his arms on his chest like a vampire and let the horrible reality of his situation slowly choke the life out of him.

That was all the invitation panic needed. He clawed at the door, seeking a sliver of space to slip a finger into, praying for his eyes to adjust to the gloom and discover a razor-thin shaft of light at a loose hinge. But of course there was nothing, and his clawing had no effect. He took to screaming, but that was bad —unbearably loud in the small space. Made him feel a thousand miles deep inside the earth, so he stopped. But the fitful clawing and scraping and scratching continued for some time.

He might have blinked out for a while then. The safe had landed at an incline, so blood was rushing to his head. It was hard to separate the blackened stillness of his steel womb from what might have been a brief period of unconsciousness. Or even an extended blackout. Why should he have thought he'd only nodded off for a short time? Maybe a day had passed without his knowledge. The thought wanted to grow into another fit, but this time he was able to resist. There was no way he was going down that road again.

He sensed movement. The safe was being hauled up. Had to be two people on the job, at least. Yet there was no chatter, no crunching of boots on the stony path. Even before he started up his screaming again, he realized the safe was soundproof.

It was difficult to judge what direction he was heading in, felt like the safe was floating and bobbing in the air by magic. Maybe Duffer was taking it to the house. It wasn't much use out in the yard, after all. Or maybe he'd sold it to Tuck Wagner down the road and they were walking the safe to Tuck's pickup. Or ...

The pond.

Of course. Duffer had caught himself another boy, so why not dump the safe into the pond? Good riddance to bad rubbish. *Oh God!* How could this be happening? As if his situation wasn't bad enough, now he saw that it could easily get a whole lot worse. Even if the pond water wasn't able to find a way in, knowing he was not only trapped in the safe but also had a body of water pressing in on him from above ... He tried desperately to take his thoughts in another direction, but it was like wading through the sludge of a nightmare.

The sensation of falling, followed by a slowing, then a wobbly descent that ended when the safe hit something hard and immovable. A rock at the bottom of the pond? It felt like when Lyndon's dad had backed the minivan into a light pole in the grocery store parking lot: unexpected and halting. Luckily the safe remained on its back. Lyndon might have lost his mind completely if it had spun around so that the door was pressed against the bottom of the pond.

A curiosity about self-destruction startled him then. What real choice did he have? He couldn't just wait for unconsciousness, could he? How long would that take? Then again, how would he kill himself? A hopeless panic tapped him on the shoulder once more. This time it was put off by a new sensation, something wet near his hairline. He ran a finger over the spot, then brought his finger to his nose. No scent. He licked it. Water. A mad giggle escaped his lips, but when a second drop struck his forehead, quickly followed by a third, he remembered it was nothing to get enthused about.

His hands shot up to the door of the safe and he pushed with every gram of his diminishing strength. Did it give just a little? He let it go, then redoubled his efforts. It did rise some, in the top right corner. Not a lot, but enough to put a bandage on his despair. He let the heavy door settle back down, and again he pushed against it, this time with gritted teeth and an animal groan. A slight metallic *pop* sounded and the dripping water grew to a trickle. He repeated the simple operation until, at last, one hinge came free.

It was a crappy development, in a way. He now stood a chance of pushing the door outward and cranking it open enough on its other hinge to allow his escape. But if he wasn't quick about it, or if it got stuck part way, the waters of Duffer's pond would rush into the small cavity of the safe—and, soon after, his lungs. A good splash had already got him across the cheek when he knocked the one hinge loose. He didn't need a second reminder.

Brute force seemed like the only solution. He'd read recently, in one of his paperbacks from the school's mail-order book program, about a little girl who'd been able to lift a motorcycle off her dad because adrenaline gave her muscles a boost when she saw him pinned, limp and bloody, under the thing, not half a block from their home. According to the same story, most accidents happened within five miles of a victim's front door. That part fit Lyndon's situation. Duffer Kendrick's farm wasn't three miles from his place. And if that part of the story applied to him, why couldn't the part about having superhuman strength for a few seconds?

No use thinking about it. The adrenaline pumping through him might not last forever. It was now or never.

For an instant he wished the safe had landed upright. It would have been easier to put some momentum into the job that way. But there also would have been the risk of knocking the safe onto its front, sealing him in an underwater tomb. He'd have to work with what he had. With a lunging motion he slammed both hands into the door above him and kept pushing until water streamed, then poured, in. Still, he kept exerting himself against the cold, wet steel. His fingers found the gap and wrapped themselves around the door's edge. He grunted with the effort of pushing even harder. There was light now, drifting down from the pond's idle surface. It wasn't much, but enough to give Lyndon the encouragement he needed to see his task through. With one mighty outpouring of force, and a deep breath of stale air, he twisted himself onto his knees and forced the door out of his way, turning it on its remaining hinge. It rotated like the cover plate of an old-fashioned peephole.

Once the gap was wide enough, he dragged himself through. Freedom at last. But he came to a halt, still feet from the surface. Something had him. Looking down through the cloudy water he saw that one of his shoelaces had snagged on the ruined hinge of the safe. He wondered if his efforts had been for nothing, but a fierce yank tore the lace free, and Lyndon floated to the surface, aided by the quickest paddling his shod feet and clothed body would allow.

Breaking through the algae skim atop the pond was like being born into a second phase of life, one he hadn't been convinced he'd live to enjoy a minute or two ago. From this point in time—paddling in the middle of Duffer's pond and gasping for air—he would take nothing for granted, let no opportunity go unexplored. It may have been the first vow he'd ever made to himself.

His focus was on staying afloat and getting to shore, but he soon noticed two men sitting on a log up along the gulch that wound through those parts. Their backs were to him and they sat too far off to hear his splashing and wheezing.

Ten feet from the bank, the toes of his shoes swept up silt from the pond floor, and then he was standing. There must have been a sharp drop-off behind him, which would explain how he and the safe had sunk so far before reaching the pond's bottom, and how the two men on the log could have carried the load far enough out to make sure it went good and deep.

The one on the left was Kendrick. The other one looked like Tuck Wagner, and Lyndon now saw a turd-brown pickup parked near the house. Definitely Tuck's. He approached with tiger stealth. Once in earshot he was able to duck behind a fat cottonwood and listen as Duffer talked Tuck's ear off.

"Well, this cocksucker said he was out, didn't have anymore. I said, 'I drove a hundred and fifty miles to this gun show, it's day one, nine-thirty a.m., and you want me to believe you're sold out of the safe I came here to buy? There's a name for that,' I told him. 'It's called false advertising. The ad said the Windsor 580 would be available for two hundred and fifty bucks. Now, I want me one of them gun safes.'

"Boy, he looked at me like he wished someone would come along and lop his fool head off. Anything to get out of this one. Finally, he offered to sell me the floor model. 'Ain't got no shelves,' I says. 'Be happy to mail you some,' he fires back.

"Hell, I was tired of arguing with the guy, so I took it."

"And why'd we just dump the damn thing in the middle of your pond?" Tuck said, cocking a thumb over his shoulder.

"Turned out some pieces were missing, along with the shelves. Wasn't good for anything besides snaring a child. So that's what I used it for. You only *heard* it fall over from inside the house, but I *saw* it. And I saw what made it fall."

Tuck gave Duffer a blank look. "You're shittin' me."

Lyndon couldn't see Duffer's face, but there was a long pause, followed by hoarse laughter as Duffer Kendrick slapped his knee and said, "Boy, you're dumber than you look, and I wouldn't have thought that was possible. Course there wasn't no one in that safe. What do you think I am, the nut who's been snatching up kids? Must have fallen over from the wind. The guy never sent the shelves, or the key. I have no way of opening the damn thing."

But Lyndon didn't buy it. He had a feeling the first thing out of Duffer's mouth had been the truth, and he suspected there were other children lying at the bottom of the pond, less fortunate than he was, feeding the fishes. His stomach turned at the thought of the water currently chilling him to the core having microscopic bits of human flesh in it.

A jagged shard of scoria caught his eye. He stooped down to snatch it up and stepped out of hiding. Finally Tuck took notice of Lyndon's presence, but it was too late to do him—or Duffer—any good. Lyndon ran for Duffer and delivered a heavy blow to the back of the man's head with the ruddy rock. It knocked him clean off the log, but Lyndon didn't stop there. He straddled Duffer's chest and drove the scoria chunk repeatedly into the man's forehead, cheeks, and eyes.

Duffer tried to resist at first, but he'd been taken by surprise, and before long he was too weak to fight back. Soon he was completely still. Only then did Lyndon rise up from his grisly work to see what Tuck thought of it all.

The man stood several feet behind Lyndon, his face a stretched piece of leather.

"Not much of a friend, huh?" Lyndon asked, short of breath.

"Why's that, son?"

"Well, you didn't exactly come to the creep's aid."

"No. No, I suppose I didn't. And I'll have to live with that, just like you'll have to live with what you done. Better hand over the rock, son."

Lyndon tossed him the scoria.

"Can I give you a lift somewhere, boy? That's my pickup right over there."

"No," Lyndon said, and he turned to walk away.

But he only made it three or four paces before he felt the impact of something striking the base of his skull. He turned and fell onto his back, then saw Tuck pitch the rock toward the pond before scooping him up in his arms and walking him to the passenger side of his pickup.

"Like I said, boy, you'll have to live with what you done. But not for long. We're going to take us a little ride over to my place, you and me. Why, I have a cellar that just goes on and on. You'll love it. Might even have a few of your old chums buried down there."

The sound of the passenger door closing against Lyndon's shoulder, followed by Tuck's footsteps as he stomped around to the other side of the vehicle, was almost as bad as the door of the safe sealing him in. Maybe every bit as bad and he was just too damn tired and hurt for it to register completely.

Tuck Wagner slid behind the wheel and turned over the engine. "You and I'll get on just fine if you keep your mouth shut while I drive. I'm none too happy about having to come back here later to clean up your little mess. But first things first." He knuckled Lyndon hard in the temple.

A wave of nausea rippled through the boy's guts, but he fell asleep before he could tell if he puked or not.

When he woke up, the pickup was climbing over the top of the last hill before Tuck's turnoff. He touched his shirt, which was bumpy with dried vomit. The sun was low, almost gone, and it cast an eerie glow on the scene below. Tuck slammed the brake pedal to the floor and brought the pickup to a jerky, angled stop on the shoulder. He stepped out to survey a small crowd that was gathered at the base of the hill, blocking the highway with its lumbering presence.

"Wagner!" one of them hollered in a hoarse, garbled voice.

And then they began to point.

Tuck took a few steps in their direction, about to speak, but then he must have realized what he was seeing. Lyndon recognized some of them as boys who'd gone missing in recent months, which meant the mass of pointing, shambling figures was made up of Tuck's victims, impossible as that was. Only, Tuck Wagner must have been at his work longer than anyone realized, because there were at least a dozen figures down there.

Tuck stood dead still for a while, like he was considering killing them all again, tearing them limb from limb with his bare hands. But terror and revulsion appeared to win out, for those still wearing skin wore only mangled strips of it, and their deathly smell came ahead of them. Tuck jumped back into the pickup, but by now Lyndon had gotten out. As Lyndon watched

Tuck peel away, back in the direction of Kendrick's farm, he felt safe at last. The dead boys were no longer pointing but beckoning with slowly curling fingers. He couldn't imagine what they wanted with him, but it wasn't bound to be any worse than what Tuck had had in mind. In fact, he felt sure it was something altogether different. Something new.

And so he walked down the hill to meet the boys, and together they all followed the setting sun into night—bloodthirsty without exception.

THE INTERVIEW

The guard led Winslow down a long corridor that made him feel as if he were inside a giant machine. In a sense, that's exactly what Stankmoor Prison was. A hungry machine that swallowed what it fancied and spat out what it found indigestible.

"Okay, Winslow." The guard's voice echoed. "Through this door coming up on the right."

The guard paused to unlock the door and ushered Winslow through to another corridor, much shorter and narrower than the first. At the far end was yet another door. He stopped halfway to this one and put a hand on Winslow's shoulder.

"You have an hour, if you care to use it. I'll be watching every move. There will be no personal contact. The interview will be conducted through Plexiglass. You ready?"

Winslow nodded.

"Let's go, then."

A lock seemed superfluous on this door, since, after unlocking it, the guard still had to use his considerable strength to release the interior bolts from their socket by manhandling a lever that never could have been shiny and new. Had anything in this place?

Winslow soon found himself facing a row of eight interview stations, like teller windows at a bank, only lower to the ground for serious sit-down palaver. No thirty-second cash withdrawals here.

"Go to window three. The prisoner will be brought in

shortly."

The guard retreated to the rear wall and crossed his arms.

Winslow sat down and waited. He'd always imagined that a place like this could make a novelist of man, or a philosopher. Since arriving at Stankmoor, however, he suspected that the dingy walls, strict routines, and bad company inspired most men to nothing more than violence and insanity.

A door banged open on the other side of the partition, and he looked up to see the prisoner being escorted in, cuffed hands jutting from the sleeves of his orange jumper. He was a small man, smaller than Winslow remembered from the trial. His hair had grown out since then, too. It hung in a cocky arc across his face.

After the man sat down across from him it was obvious that Winslow would have to be the one to get things started. The prisoner fidgeted and avoided eye contact.

"Thanks for agreeing to this. I know it's not easy." It was all Winslow could think to say through the speaking holes in the Plexiglass.

"I was curious." One corner of the man's mouth lifted in an odd half smile as he spoke.

"Yeah." Essays had flooded through Winslow's mind regarding questions he would ask and reprimands he would dole out if he finally got the chance to interrogate this man. Faced with the reality of it, he felt like an adolescent on a first date. "I suppose I want to get a better sense of why you did what you did. And I guess I want you to know a little something about the woman you killed. Her memory deserves that much. I'm not here for an apology. I wouldn't accept one."

The prisoner's head slid methodically forward and back in a noncommittal nod. His thin lips were set in a grim expression.

"She was my wife, of course," Winslow continued. "You know that. But you don't know what kind of wife she was."

"I'm sure she was the greatest wife in the world."

"I wouldn't know. She's the only one I ever had." He was

surprised at how unaffected he was by the prisoner's barb, but what more could this man possibly take from him? "She had her faults, though. I used to hate the way she flirted with every man at every party we ever attended. Her snooty attitude about anything to do with sports. That kind of thing.

"But that must not have been real hatred, huh? You must know a whole other category of hate, because Sharon pissed me off plenty of times, and I never so much as laid a finger on her. She did nothing to you, and ..."

Silence prevailed for a moment.

"It's catching, isn't it," the prisoner remarked.

Timothy Barnes, he was called. So young to be against the world. But it was usually the young who were given the strongest passions and the least wisdom to control them.

He was right. It *was* catching. Winslow thought he'd been through all the anger he had in him. He'd waited to request this interview until equanimity had gained some sway in his life, but in an instant, like a sick man coughing spittle into his face, Barnes had planted a seed of hostility in Winslow, who hoped the mind had its own kind of immune system.

"What do you do with it in here, your anger, your rage? Who do you take it out on with no innocent women around?"

"Life's different in here. You live closer to the edge, all the time. There's more fear in this place than anger. I mean, every now and then there's a fistfight, but those are more for entertainment than anything."

"What about rape?"

"What about it?"

"Is it a problem?"

"Not like in the comic books, chief, but I could tell you a couple of stories. You get desperate for companionship in here. Some guys crack under the hopelessness of it. Some turn to God in a big way, which seems like tipping the hangman to me, but whatever. Others get tired of whacking off into the toilet while their bunkmate pretends to be asleep, so they go on the prowl."

"Have you ever been ..."

"Prowled? I see, you want to know that I've suffered good and plenty for what I did to your wife. You're sick, you know that?"

Winslow wouldn't have consciously put it in such plain terms, but he supposed that was exactly what he wanted to know.

"You didn't rape my wife. Why not?"

Barnes's expression changed. He looked down at the narrow shelf in front of him. Was he deciding how to answer or doing his best to disregard Winslow? It was impossible to tell.

"Not good enough for you?"

"I'm no fuckin' rapist, okay? It was supposed to be a simple burglary. We were through all of this in court. I don't see—"

"But you never took the stand. You just kind of slouched in safety between your attorneys, like a coward. I want to hear it from you. That's why I'm here. Are you sticking to that story? Did Sharon wake up and surprise you, so you had to cut her open? A stab wound maybe I could understand. But you sliced her up like ... Dear God, like I don't know what. What was driving you?"

"I haven't quite come to that myself, Mr. Winslow. I've done my share of B-and-Es. Some of them have involved scuffles, but that night in your house was different."

"Different how?"

"I don't know. Your wife came at me, you know? With a lot of attitude. Cursing me up and down, just fucking fearless. Told me to get the hell out of her house before she caved my head in with a lamp. That's just how she said it. Didn't threaten to call the cops, like most people would. She threatened to fucking kill me.

"I guess I'm not used to taking that kind of shit from a woman. It didn't sit right with me. Something snapped. I mean, she wouldn't shut up, and before you know it, I saw how the night was going to end."

Winslow shook his head but didn't take his eyes off Barnes. "Well, that certainly fills in some gaps for me."

The sonofabitch actually smiled.

"Now maybe I can fill in a gap or two for you."

"How's that, chief?"

"I know you're not married. There are a lot of stupid women in the world, but I have yet to meet one who would reduce herself to calling *you* husband."

Barnes's face gathered at the center, making Winslow appreciate the barrier between them.

"Still, you have family. You're actually something of a family *man*, aren't you? Your Aunt Millie apparently means quite a lot to you. Your sister Ann and her boy Jake. Well, hardly a boy anymore, but that's what you still call him, isn't it?"

Barnes leaned in close to the Plexiglas. "What have you been up to, Mr. Winslow?"

"Don't worry, I was far more civilized than you. A single bullet to the head of each one. That's all it took. I didn't feel the need to kick them when they were down, or start carving into them. I just ended their lives and walked away." He smiled and stood up, watching Barnes begin to tremble and redden. "Thanks for this time together, Timothy. I've enjoyed it, but I better get back to Phoenix so I can turn myself in. Or maybe I'll kill myself. I haven't decided yet, but it's a long drive back. I'll have plenty of time to make up my mind."

As he asked to be led back to the main gate, Winslow could hear Timothy Barnes behind him, yelling for a guard to let him make a phone call. It made him laugh a little as he followed his guide back through the maze of Stankmoor's innards.

He stepped into the vise-like heat of another southern Arizona day in midsummer, crossed the melting parking lot to his sun-faded coupe, and started down the frontage road to the main highway. After several miles, he skidded the car onto the shoulder, squirting pebbles and dust into the parched air. He slammed his fist against the steering wheel, again and again. He knew he wouldn't be able to hold back sobs, even before his body began to shake. His haughty pride melted into an open display of sorrow and grief. He threw his arms across his chest, hugged himself as tears streamed out of his eyes, and rocked slowly back and forth.

It had all been a lie. He never could have let himself sink to Barnes's level like that, not in a million years. Allowed to get his hands around the sonofabitch's throat, he wasn't sure what he might be capable of. But the man's family? Never. He'd merely done the research.

The lie had been petty, and its effects would be temporary, but the bastard would never forget what it had felt like to slip inside Winslow's skin for a spell. Nothing could ever bring Sharon back, but she damn sure would have appreciated this.

He wiped his cheeks dry with his sleeves and gunned it back onto the road.

THE OCULIST'S DILEMMA

The view shouldn't matter to him, but it does. From his perch, high up where two crooked palm trees touch to form an X, Dr. Hochens watches the still blue sea. The billion glimmering jewels upon its surface, mere refractions of sunlight, want to lull him into a trance, but he resists. One way or another, the last moments of his life are playing out on this wretched island. He determines to experience them wide eyed and aware, if not exactly full of gratitude.

An afternoon breeze slackens and the sun warms his bare back. He closes his eyes to savor the simple pleasure. His first day on the island—only two days prior—was hard but bearable. He soon made peace with the fact that he would die of dehydration, or starvation, eventually. At least he wouldn't live to know the disintegration of his vision, layer by layer, shade by shade, until he was left completely blind.

But then, this morning, a simple hike. He nearly tripped and fell into the natural pool, which was hiding around a bend in the rough path that two rows of lush trees were marking out for him. Squatting beside the water and cupping his hands to bring a scoopful to his mouth, he almost hoped it would turn out to be a saltwater spring, fed from below by the ocean itself. That would have been an end to it.

But he didn't blanch as the cool water cascaded down his throat, because there was no salt. Only refreshing, life-giving water. Which meant his most immediate obstacle to longevity was overcome. Hunger, on the other hand, would take its time with him. He'd been nibbling on a few of the island plants and didn't seem to be getting sick from them, but he knew he would need more than succulents and berries in the long run.

A rustling sound arose amid the ferns at the rim of the pool, first from one location, then another. He noticed a smell, too, like the vinegar odor of damp, dead leaves on the verge of rot. His imagination convinced him he was picking up the scent of animals—those responsible for the noise—of oily and matted fur. After a last hurried slurp of delicious water, he stood and backed away, the sounds coming from everywhere by then. Arcing around, widdershins, he found his forward gear at last and fled the strange oasis.

Now, seated at the juncture of the two palms, he watches as seabirds wheel in the cloudless sky. Whatever is crawling around below, he wants no part of it. The urge to drink will grow strong enough, he supposes, that he will brave the scurrying things again. But what truly bothers him is that he can't help wondering what they might taste like, though he has yet to spot, let alone catch, one. He imagines them to be a variant of the rat, larger and with undiscovered appetites, having made do with so little for so long.

His stomach turns.

One last solo yachting adventure while I can still see to pilot a boat. Was that so much to ask?

He was careful in choosing his lookout, not wanting to face the sun. In part it is habit, from years of lecturing patients on the importance of protecting their eyes. It is also a mental shield, however thin, that might help keep his own encroaching darkness at bay.

The longer he waits, though, the more he risks having fate make his final decisions for him. He will fall from the trees eventually: out of lightheadedness or fatigue, or by accident. Then what? The scurrying rat-variants will sniff him out in seconds, be on him in an instant. The pain will be bad. The wet sounds of their feasting might be worse.

But what if there is another way? There *is* another way! And better to act while there's still light in the sky, for he knows he'll lose all nerve once the sun goes down. He clambers down the curving trunk of one of the trees, jumping the last couple of feet to the soft earth below. A high-pitched chittering starts up all around him and he runs with all his might. Through brush and over fallen trees. Across the pristine sands that mantle the island's most expansive beach, to the shallows beyond. He dives into the water, and swims.

Having paddled out as far as he can manage with his diminished strength, he turns back to behold the island. A slight laugh escapes him, then another, louder and raspier than the first. Soon he is laughing like a madman. Laughing at the island, at his pre-moribund eyes, at the unseen rat-variants. At God, in fact, who always has the very best jokes.

"Fuck you!" he calls out to the island. "I'm not going to die on your soil. I've escaped. You hear me, escaped!" Again he laughs.

A dark line appears where foliage meets sand, moving— *gliding*—to the water's edge, like a serpent whose movements aren't quite right. And the line is only the beginning. Behind it comes a carpet of writhing, teeming life. His instincts have been good. They *are* ratlike, and large as house cats. As they march toward the water's edge, he can see the sun glinting off their sharp white teeth.

He lets himself slip beneath the surface, his mouth drawing open. It is time. But almost as soon as he is under, he feels himself being buoyed back up to the surface, helped along, as if on some kind of raft. Only when he is back on the beach, coughing up water, does he make out that the rat-variants have combined forces to form a living flotation device and deliver him back to shore.

Their intent as they circle, however, is not to help the shipwrecked ophthalmologist. It is to feed.

Relenting, Dr. Hochens stares into the sun, and suffers his

implacable fate.

IN THE CHILLEST LAND

J ackson stood up, sat down, stood again. His joints popped
with each movement. At least it was less frigid down here,
out of the swirling wind. And at least his fall hadn't wedged
him in the crevasse. He'd been lucky enough to follow the me-
andering tunnel of blue ice to a hole that dropped him into the
den in which he was now trapped. From the hole to the floor
of the compartment had been a drop of about twelve feet, but
he was fit enough to endure that. He'd made it up this goddamn
mountain, after all. He'd been training all his life for a crack at
McKinley. Now this.

"Denali," his climbing partner, Ejaz, had corrected him a
thousand times on the way up.

"You say Denali, I say McKinley," Jackson would respond
without fail. Ejaz would shake his head and smile.

It was mostly a matter of keeping fear from taking over.
He had some food in his pack, which fortunately hadn't torn
away from his body during the chaotic descent. He even had
a small butane stove for warming food and melting snow. Ejaz
knew where Jackson was, roughly, so there was hope for a happy
ending to all of this. It was morning, and as the day advanced,
light would come in through the hole. Not much, perhaps, but
enough to keep him sane. Night would come eventually, but by
then he'd be found.

It had probably been a mistake to backtrack to the

Kahiltna Glacier on his own. No, it *had* been. He could admit that to himself now, for all the good it did him. He'd roused Ejaz in the wee hours to tell him he intended to do a solo scout of the West Rib, which was much trickier than the heavily trodden West Buttress route they were pursuing together. To his astonishment, Ejaz hadn't put up much resistance to the idea.

As he'd plodded across the glacier's Northeast Fork, the clutching wind dusting his balaclava with icy grit and howling in his ears, his thoughts drifted to the Japanese explorer Naomi Uemura, who had scaled this very mountain all alone, with bamboo poles rigged onto his shoulders to prevent a nasty fall if he stumbled into a hidden crevasse. It had always seemed like overkill to Jackson. Not anymore.

And now Ejaz will have a hell of a time finding you ...

He guessed the den to be roughly twenty-five feet in diameter. To test the estimate he walked a straight line, one arm outstretched, the other gripping his pack. When his gloved hand met with the wall, he dropped the pack and began edging his way along the perimeter of the ice chamber. He felt a little like the character in Poe's "The Pit and the Pendulum," and for the first time since slipping into the blind crack of ice dozens of feet above he felt a twinge of relief. Even if starvation and cold battled over the rights to his mortal coil, he was unlikely to end up in straits as dire as those of Poe's hapless hero.

Then he heard a noise.

A soft *fsht, fsht* from across the chamber. He froze. Only enough daylight seeped in from above to give the center of the cavern a vague nimbus of visibility. His mind raced for possible explanations for the sound, which refused to repeat itself for the longest time. Animal life was all he could think of, but it staggered the mind. What could possibly dwell in such conditions? It would have to be avian at this altitude. But what?

fsshhht, fsshhht

Something shuffling across the ice to him. His heart slammed against his chest wall like a jackhammer, faster and faster. The sound of lips parting. He squeezed his eyes shut and began to shake. Silence. He let his face relax but kept his eyes closed. What was that smell? Wet dog?

He couldn't take it anymore. Not knowing was too much. His eyes fluttered open, and before him was the slack face of something vulpine, distrust and curiosity aflame in the recesses of its eyes. The thing's protruding jaw hung wide, grinding slowly from side to side. A wave of stinking air issued from its mouth, and Jackson had to fight back vomit.

Tink

He swiveled his head to the left.

Tink

Now to the right.

It had hooked its claws into the ice wall behind him, barring his escape. Hope was gone. Surely he had lost his mind. He slid down the wall to a sitting position and noticed that the creature was enormous and covered with alternating patches of thick fur and ugly sores where no hair could grow. He pressed his eyes closed, opened them. Not a hallucination, still there. It had tilted its head down at him and was snickering, or so it seemed. Then it pushed away from the wall, taking a couple of steps back, on hind legs only.

"Who …" It was useless. Jackson had no voice, and there were no words anyway.

The thing turned and ran to the center of the room, directly beneath the opening Jackson had fallen through. It was larger than he'd realized when it was up close and stooped over. Fully extended it must have cleared eight feet. Reddish hair straggled from its scalp in sparse clumps. It paused to look at him, but it was still too dark to read its expression from that distance.

Reaching up casually with one almost-human arm, it grasped the edge of the hole and hauled itself out of sight. A banshee wail—and the *tink, tink, tink* of nails in the ice—trailed away. Jackson was left waiting for its inevitable return, though thankful to be alive.

His eyes refused to pull away from the gaping hole, which

was almost perfectly round, but his mind reverted to studying his regrets, for it was in no condition to take in what he had witnessed.

Why had he left his battery-powered lamp with Ejaz, who had dropped his the day before and cracked open the bulb? Extra batteries they had packed. Extra bulbs they had not. He figured the ice cave was about as illuminated as it was going to get by the sunlight that trickled in. It wasn't enough. If ever in his life he'd needed a flashlight it was now. Not that what it showed him would be so great—especially if the strange animal kept scraps of whatever it ate in this cave—but a little light could do wonders for the faculties.

He felt for his pack and resumed his groping assessment of the perimeter, every now and then glancing at the opening, half expecting to see the thing's leering face at the hole, hands gripping the edge like a demonic Kilroy. But it didn't return. He wondered what it was doing. Hunting? What could it possibly ...

"Oh god," he muttered. "Ejaz. Help! *Ejaz, get away! Help!*"

Here I go, he thought. *Carrying on like a madman.*

He recognized the futility of his screams but kept on calling out as he proceeded along the wall, until his foot struck something that stopped him cold.

Even through his thick boots and woolen socks he could tell what he'd kicked, partly by the slight resistance of the object and partly by the sound it made as it skittered across the icy floor. The horror of his situation began to sink in. His defenses were depleted, and he sank once again to the floor. He had kicked a bone. Human, he easily imagined. Possibly a femur. Something good sized, at any rate.

He tugged off his crusted-over balaclava, goggles, and climbing gloves, then cried a little. There was so much he didn't understand about the world. More than he'd ever thought possible, apparently. And it wasn't the ice-dwelling monster that troubled him the most, he was surprised to discover. It was Jenna. Jenna, who'd asked him for a deeper commitment a thousand times. He had stubbornly refused. Some macho part of him insisted that even telling her he loved her would give her a level of control that could never be won back. Of course, he'd had it all wrong. What could never be undone was the simple fact that he loved her more than the moon and the stars. And she loved him. And the only thing standing in the way of their lasting happiness was three unutterable words ... and a mountain-dwelling terror.

"I love you," he managed through tears. Of course he did. How clearly he felt it now. How strongly he loved life, the world, his friends and family. How deeply he yearned for a second chance to prove he was guided by the will to help others and rise through life by the toil of his own two hands.

She'd called him a selfish brute for going on this expedition. He wasn't sure she'd have him back if he did make it out alive, but he was determined to find out. If he not only got free of this stinking den but managed to evade capture at the hands of whatever thing called this mountain home, he would spend his life in service of his feelings for Jenna and those most dear to him.

Ejaz, he thought ruefully. And his sorrow gave way to exhaustion.

*   *   *

"Sonofabitch," Ejaz mumbled into his balaclava as he planted the crampons of his left boot firmly into the incline of ice. "Leaves me with a glorified flashlight and goes on his merry way. As if one little act of generosity will make up for his thoughtlessness. Prick."

He didn't mean a word of it, but it felt good to let anger have the moment. The longer he could put off worrying himself sick about his friend and climbing partner the better. Still, it was not an ideal way to start the day, waking to find that your partner had given you the slip in order to pursue whatever selfish agenda had claimed his fevered mind. Ejaz had seen the daredevil spirit in climbers before, the unending drive to outdo all those who had gone before, to take the more dangerous course. Not only to summit the mountain, but to do it on the edge of a razor. Jackson had never hinted that he would try something this stupid, but Ejaz guessed it right away upon waking. The constant barrage of questions on the way up, about how many climbers had tackled the West Rib, and which ones had made the ascent without oxygen. It didn't take a detective to figure that he'd gone off to do some exploring on his own, probably by way of the Kahiltna Glacier.

And sure enough. Thanks to a downturn in the wind's ferocity, Ejaz was able to pick up Jackson's trail before reaching the glacier's Northeast Fork. The trail had led him to the steep rise he now climbed. The eastern sky was a wide flame of morning's pinks and yellows and oranges, but Ejaz had little time to enjoy the spectacular sight if he was to find his missing partner.

Soon, as the grade of his climb diminished, he could see a good distance across a gentler slope of ice and snow. Something caught his eye as he looked in that direction. A glimpse of movement, and then it was gone. It couldn't have been Jackson. Surely he'd made it much farther than this by now, unless he was delirious and traveling in circles. Ejaz waited a moment, still as a stalk, to see if he'd spot the movement again, but there was nothing. He didn't look up from the business of climbing again until he'd reached more level snowpack and was rewarded with another sighting. It was nearly human in shape but considerably larger as it loped along the horizon in the four-legged manner of an animal. Its head appeared to turn in his direction, and his blood turned as icy cold as his vast white surroundings. The thing dove between two large rock outcroppings and was gone.

What had he just seen? There was no good answer to the question, no explanation that he could think of for the existence of any living thing up here, besides Jackson and himself. He felt his skin shrink up on his bones as fear began to spread outward from his belly.

At least Jackson's boot prints resumed on the straightaway and meandered in the opposite direction of the opening where the thing had disappeared. He pressed ahead. A half hour, at least, passed without any further sightings. He glanced back at the outcroppings periodically. Nothing appeared to be tailing him.

But a touch on the shoulder sent him spinning, almost sprawling. The damn thing had circled around and caught up with him. There it was, not three feet from his face. It let out a shrill keen and stood itself up to full height. He was beyond the ability to flee and wondered absently if the thing, which had the snout of a wild dog or hyena, would be disappointed that he was such easy prey. The look in its eyes and the foaming saliva that dripped from razor-like canines gave the impression that it didn't much care, which was his last observation before being thumped on the head with one of its heavy paws and dropping from consciousness.

*　*　*

His vision was still gone as other senses awakened. He sensed motion, being dragged on his back. Did someone have him by the collar? Yes, he could hear his parka scratching along on the ice. Then he remembered the misshapen dog-thing and pressed his heels into the ice as hard as he could, but his progress went unimpeded. Why couldn't he see? The last thing he needed was to panic, but if it had blinded him ...

No, it wasn't that. His balaclava had turned. He breathed more easily, but he was still in a hell of a lot of danger.

Please don't be dead, Jackson, he hoped, almost prayed.

He stopped moving. The creature released his collar, and the back of his head hit the ice, giving him stars for a moment. He quickly freed himself of the balaclava and sat up to get his bearings. It stood several yards away, eyeing him with amused interest. The hind legs were bent slightly at the knees, and the upper body leaned in at him. It was enormous, its coat long and flowing reddish brown in the cold wind, despite numerous ugly patches of bare skin all over its body. The effect was both repulsive and extraordinary. What the hell *was* this thing?

It seemed proud, and he wondered what it had to be so goddamn proud of. He meant to lean back on his hands, maybe even ask it a question or two, but his hands didn't touch ice or snow behind him, only kept going down until he figured out what was up and caught himself. Looking back he saw that he'd been dropped at the edge of a wicked crevasse. He scurried away from its yawning blueness, more scared than ever of the reckless creature now, and shot to his feet to issue a challenge before he could lose his nerve. But he never had a chance. It was on him in an instant, growling in his face, filling his nostrils with noisome breath, and raking its claws at his shoulders and chest. His shock and terror left him unequal to the task of resistance, so when it gave him a push he was little more than dead weight.

Down he slid into the crevasse for what seemed like forever—feet first one moment, head first the next—with no way of gauging what obstacles or pitfalls might be approaching, but eventually his fall came to an end, and not the brutal end he'd expected. He wasn't impaled on a spire or wedged inextricably in a stone pocket. He simply fell through a hole and landed on a floor of ice.

"All right, you bastard," he heard someone say in a crazed voice. "Let's settle things right now."

"Jackson?" Ejaz whispered.

"Ejaz?" It was a dry, husky response.

Jackson approached from the shadows, and Ejaz could hardly believe it was the same man he'd begun this expedition with. His climbing partner's usually explosive blond hair was matted down close to his scalp, and he looked weak, on the verge of collapse. Still, it was a happy reunion for two men with so much yet to work out if they planned on living to see another day. They embraced heartily, once Ejaz was able to convince his back to let him stand up.

"I wondered if I'd see you again," Jackson said.

"The question had crossed my mind as well."

"How did you find me?"

"I didn't exactly find you. I mean, I was tracking you, but … I trust you're familiar with the giant dog-creature roaming around up there?"

Jackson did his best to smile.

"Yeah," Ejaz went on, "well, it tossed me in here with you. God only knows what its plans are."

"They're not good. It has a nest in here, littered with bones. Human bones."

"Jesus Christ."

"It's given me an idea, though. Come, let's sit and talk, away from the hole."

Jackson's aversion to conversing near the opening bordered on superstitious, in Ejaz's view, considering how far down they were from the surface. Besides, did Jackson really think the creature was capable of comprehending their words? It was possible, but the thing seemed far more animal than human. Ejaz kept his thoughts to himself.

"Here, sit," Jackson said. "I'll be right back." In less than a minute he returned with a strange contraption in his arms. He joined Ejaz on the ice floor. "I figured, why let all these bones go to waste? I mean, people have died here, but it doesn't have to be in vain."

Ejaz saw that the apparatus was fashioned from bones tied together, almost in the shape of a large kite.

"I used my rappelling rope to connect everything. It's nice and tight, see?"

"I get it. The knee bone's connected to the thigh bone—"

"Are you making light of this?"

"Sorry, I'm just trying to make the best of a crap situation. What's this thing for?"

"That's what I'm getting to. I figure we can heave it up through the opening in the ceiling. You know, the long way. And once it's through, if we get it just right, it will act as a grapple."

"Christ." Ejaz leaned against the wall in disbelief. "That

thing's supposed to hold our weight?"

"Well, mine, sure. I'll run the rope through pitons in the ice for you once I'm up."

"What were you thinking, man? You're damn lucky I even thought to look for you on the Northeast Fork. We both are."

"Lucky? What are you talking about? I told you I was ... Oh, shit. You must have been answering me in your sleep. I wondered why you were so goddamn agreeable. Well let's put it behind us for now. McKinley hasn't defeated us yet, but we need to move."

"Denali," Ejaz said.

"What?"

"The mountain. It's called Denali."

This time Jackson smiled more easily. "You say Denali, I say McKinley."

"White people," Ejaz said, shaking his head jokingly from side to side.

"I still don't see how Pakistan has any skin in this game."

"Hey, us POCs have to stand together against the oppressor."

They smiled weakly at each other before digging into the task at hand. In no time, Jackson was ready to give his invention an initial toss.

"Might make some noise and echo up to the top," Ejaz said.

"Well then I'll have to throw as accurately as possible the first time."

"Yeah, I guess that's the truth. I hope to hell this works."

Jackson let the kite of bones fly. It sailed through the hole but came right back down to him.

"William Tell, you want me to give it a whirl?"

"Ha, ha. Let me have another go."

He held the rope in his left hand and underhanded the bone kite through the opening once again. This time one of the longer bones caught the edge on the way through, which caused the whole thing to wobble and rotate. It landed beside the hole, out of sight.

"Yes!" Jackson cheered, and they exchanged a high five.

"Can you get it to span the hole?"

"If I can't we're sunk."

"Fair enough. Easy does it."

Jackson pulled very gently on the rope, hand over hand, striving to keep up a fluid motion. Then, when almost half of the tied bones could be seen overhead, he yanked the rope across his chest, turning into the rapid tug with all of his weight. Ejaz thought he resembled the American soldier anchoring the flag pole into the ground in the famous Iwo Jima photograph.

"It worked!" Jackson whispered enthusiastically.

"Now you're surprised. Before, you were so sure of your handiwork."

"Well, you never know until you try. But by God, we're going to make it out of here."

Jackson took the rope in both hands, and Ejaz watched closely as he climbed toward the opening. The bone rigging flattened some with his weight, but it seemed incredibly sturdy. Jackson had always been the one you wanted on your side when something needed a knot. This sure as hell reinforced his reputation.

In what seemed like less than a minute Jackson had lifted one edge of the bone kite, as if pushing up a manhole cover, and slithered through. Once topside, he held the contraption up and peered down with a triumphant look that Ejaz thought was maybe a little premature.

"Send up the backpacks, man. Let's keep moving."

Ejaz did as he was told and Jackson drew up the rope.

"Now step back a bit."

As if showing off, Jackson pulled one strand of rope from the knot work of the grapple, and the whole thing folded in and came apart. Bones clattered to the floor of the cavern. He went about hammering pitons into the ice and running the rope through before dropping one end back down to Ejaz, who quickly made the climb and joined Jackson above the den.

They smiled at each other but reserved any further cele-
bration. It was still a good haul up the funnel-like crevasse.
They would need their ice hammers, crampons, and every
ounce of failing strength they could muster if they were to rope
themselves to the surface. And then there was the long hike
back to camp, not to mention the threat posed by the beast.
Their troubles were far from over.

Ejaz was thankful that if he had to be in this rotten
situation, at least he was in it with Jackson, who constantly as-
tounded him with his presence of mind. What could have possessed such a level-headed climber to go off on this solitary trek
in the first place?

He shook his head and followed Jackson up the dizzying
universe of varicolored ice.

* * *

It was a tiring ascent but eventually they emerged from
the crack. Jackson rested on his knees and surveyed their surroundings, while Ejaz fell onto his back, utterly spent.

Jackson could see the enemy creeping and slouching in
the distance. There was no time to waste.

* * *

"I don't like how open it is between here and the drop to
base camp," Jackson said.

Ejaz cupped his gloved hands over his nose and mouth
and expelled air to warm his face. He'd hoped his balaclava
would be waiting for him when he reached the lip of the crevasse, but it wasn't. This was all he could do to stay warm.

Something hit him from the side. He looked down and
saw Jackson's balaclava lying in the snow at his feet.

"We'll trade off wearing it," Jackson said.

Ejaz nodded his appreciation as he pulled the mask over

his head and tucked the neck piece into the shoulders of his jacket. It was brutally cold, but the wind was still down, merely dusting the snowpack with an occasional devil.

"I think we should separate a bit," Jackson continued. "If it does come for us, why give it a two-for-one special? If we stay apart and it comes for one of us, the other one might be able to step in and do some good. If not, at least he'll have a shot at securing his own safety."

Might. The word echoed in Ejaz's mind. He didn't want to put distance between them. He wanted closeness. He felt like a scared child.

"How are we going to share the mask?" he said, hoping it didn't sound desperate.

"Keep it. Just till the drop. We're so out in the open up here. From the glacier's edge to base camp we should be home free. Why don't I stick to the ridge up here. You veer around the basin. I'll keep an eye on you as we go. Sound good?"

"No, it sounds exactly like shit. But you're right."

Jackson patted him on the arm. "Of course I'm right." And he walked ahead.

Ejaz wished it hadn't felt so much like goodbye. This was no place for goodbyes.

*   *   *

Not five minutes after their parting, Jackson sensed movement at the corner of his eye and knew the end game was upon them. His muscles tensed but he didn't want to give away his awareness—to the creature or to Ejaz. He turned slowly and called out to his friend, but he was gone. Movement came again, so fast across the snowy glacier that it was nearly a blur. Jackson screamed as he realized the thing had chosen him over Ejaz. Even as he turned away he saw the futility of fleeing. There was no hope of outpacing the abomination.

Try! his brain screamed, and he pressed forward as fast as his fatigued limbs and the deep snow would allow.

A noise behind him, like someone getting the wind knocked out of him, followed by a maddened howl. He looked over his shoulder and stopped. Ejaz must have seen the attack coming and stepped in to help, because he was on top of the creature, trying desperately not to allow the situation to reverse itself. Jackson started toward them, but his progress was painfully slow. They rolled away from him in their struggle, down the backside of the ridge. They gathered speed and were soon out of sight.

"*No!*" Jackson yelled, but by the time he got as far down the other side of the ridge as he dared, he could see them tumbling over a beetling lip of mountain and freefalling into a bank of cloud cover.

He fell onto one knee, took a clump of hair in each hand, and screamed out across the Alaska Range. His screams turned to sobs, and the sobs turned inward. Soon he was weeping into his gloves. He felt sure that no thief or murderer had ever felt so low and disgusted with himself. He'd wanted a solo experience on this mountain. Now he had one. He also had a long descent to base camp and beyond to think through his guilt, to dream up ways to punish himself. Everything meaningful in his life he'd either discarded or mistreated. There'd been a moment, as he and Ejaz cleared the brim of the crevasse, when he thought maybe life had offered him a turning point. He'd started to see this whole nightmare as a second chance. But there were no more second chances. Not for him.

He considered following Ejaz and the creature into eternity. It had a certain lazy appeal to it. All it would take was a relaxing of the muscles and a few somersaults down the ridge. Gravity would take care of the rest. It would be an end to the life of self-loathing he faced, and the long hours of guilt that surely awaited him in the weeks and months to come.

But there was Jenna to consider. He'd used up a lot of second chances with her over the years, too, but maybe she'd find another one for him somewhere near the bottom of her heart. It wasn't much to go on, especially considering the state of their relationship. But as long as there was hope, no matter how dim, there was reason to press on.

Besides, if he blinked out of existence, the mystery of the Denali Monster would die with him. Someone had to find out what the hell the thing was, and whether there were more of its kind roaming the mountaintops. Maybe he'd be able to get a party together and venture back up here to explore the den. Perhaps even search for the remains of the creature, though it would mean risking the possibility of stumbling across Ejaz's preserved corpse. It was a chance he'd be willing to take if it meant learning something about the monster's origins, or saving the lives of future climbers—anything to help alleviate his guilty conscience.

But first, home.

ON THE STRANGEST SEA

His arms felt heavy as he pulled the small red door shut behind him. Climbing the steep, narrow planks from the lower cabins to the deck of *The Lonesome Buccaneer*, he noticed it in his legs, too. His whole body, in fact, behaved as if the pockets of his black leather vest, sailor's blouse, and pantaloons were weighted down with ballast. Abel Sykes was too weary to revel in his recent accomplishment, but he was determined to try. He dragged himself to the gunwale and stared beyond the bowsprit, out across the unbreakable sea before him, hoping to find a revelation in the repetition of blues, grays, and greens that stretched in every direction. Something to bring him a moment's peace before his final drastic act.

Something did come over him eventually, but it wasn't the quiet reassurance he'd been hoping for, the unshakable affirmation he sought. After an hour or more of witnessing the sea in one of her quiet lulls, he realized that something special was on its way. It was a knack that some old sea dogs picked up after too much time away from land. A sense that maybe the sea wasn't so unbreakable after all, that there was a universe of constant change beneath the surface, no matter how calm it appeared from above—and maybe some particle of that flux was thinking of breaking free, or laboring at it even now.

Never had a calmer sea borne him across its glassy top, and he couldn't have put it in stronger terms than that, it being his twenty-eighth year on one whaling vessel or another. Not a cloud in the sky, either. Conditions were maybe a little too perfect. Sykes knew the manner of an ocean about to be breached by a sperm whale. He'd seen the hesitant lunge preceding the arrival of a monstrous cetacean many times. And he'd observed the upwelling of cool waters from beneath warm. This wasn't like either of those phenomena. This was a swell so sweeping and vast he could have sworn he heard the drifting timbers of the *Buccaneer* and her two flanking whaleboats groan in response, though she was a clear two-and-a-half knots from whatever was pushing all that water skyward.

And then it broke. A rolling arc of gray flesh, as long as an armada of frigates moored prow to stern, and considerably thicker. That was only what he could see of it. Some considerable portion had returned to the depths before he could make any sense of what he was witnessing. He let a deep shudder pass through him before calling to the deckhands to alert them to the fact that they were headed straight for the most immense creature of the sea that Abel Sykes had ever set eyes on. It was a momentary lapse. There was no one to hear his hollering. He was alone.

He did what he could to batten down and tie back sails, but it was beyond the endurance and speed of one man. Periodically he allowed himself a glimpse of the ponderous movement of the thing that refused to reveal either end of itself. *The Lonesome Buccaneer* was without a helmsman, and she pitched violently in the worsening tumult. Abel had expected to die on her deck this very day, or by jumping off of it, but now curiosity had him by the throat. The creature, it was clear, continued to glide from where it had emerged to where it was returning, rolling gently as it did so. It was no whale. That was certain. But how large could the thing possibly be? Where was the end of it? Abel was transfixed.

He imagined the hand of Captain Fulsome gripping his shoulder. "If you have any ideas about what that might be, Sykes, I'd love to hear them," the captain might have said in his guttural yet clipped voice. It always had the uncanny ability to cut through the roar of any storm, that voice. Designed not only to be heard but obeyed.

"No sir," Abel said out loud, seeing little difference between the real and the imagined as he watched the impossibility of the sea creature on the move. "I ran out of ideas at least a hundred yards ago. She just keeps coming. I've never seen anything like it."

That's when the suspense ended and the terror began, for when the great gray monster finally did come to an end, it was no tailfin that could be seen following the rest of its bulk under the surface. It was simply a tip—as if belonging to a tentacle that something was fanning in the water. But if that was the case, how vast was the rest of the creature?

Sykes stared into the nonexistent eyes of his make-believe captain, seeking comfort, or at least reassurance. Then came a long stillness, and any seaman Abel knew would have testified to the fact that there's a certain kind of lull on the open sea that's far worse than the most tempestuous squall of lashing rain and ripping wind. All that could be done now was to wait for unbending Fate to rush in and break apart the silence and dread.

Was the thing grinning, down in its unknowable domain, aware that the longer it held any onlookers in thrall of what was to come, the greater would be the shock of its full emergence from the sea? Abel sensed this was so.

The first hint of the actual magnitude of the beast came not from the horizon, where Abel's eyes were trained, but from directly below. As if Neptune had the sloop on a chain and now gave it a tug, down dropped *The Lonesome Buccaneer*. It was a considerable drop, too, but more considerable still was that the ship never plunged beneath the surface. The water in her immediate vicinity had fallen along with the vessel.

There was barely time to register this odd phenomenon before the horizon claimed his attention once more. As if the very world were giving birth to a new moon, a bell of ferocious water rose up from the deep. Immense waterfalls cascaded from the thing that rose and pulsed in the aroused sea. Its dimensions were dizzying, because if something could be this enormous, what did that say about the actual size of things as Abel had been perceiving them since infancy? Was all judgment relative, or so easily shattered?

The time for marveling over such things was soon over, though, for what goes down must come up, and up shot the *Buccaneer* as the water reacted again to the expulsion of the beast, rippling in gigantic waves, any one of which would have been the most impressive sight of Abel's life twenty minutes ago. Not anymore. Now all was insignificant in the face of the sea-dwelling wonder.

Timbers cracked, then snapped. A deafening report echoed from below deck, and the *Buccaneer* lurched forward. She was coming apart at the seams, and suddenly Abel was flying toward the creature, launched into the spume-filled air by a twisting wrench of undercurrent that doomed *The Lonesome Buccaneer* to a dark, wet grave. Fate was closing in as he tumbled through the air.

He had no choice but to breathe deeply of the ocean's salt. It loomed so large now, the thing from below, that it brooked absolutely no comparison to anything from Abel's world. Little waterfalls—only fifty feet in length by this time—still dribbled from its lowest regions, but it appeared to be mostly free of the water, and its shape was as clear as such an amorphous thing was likely to get. Abel had been right about the tentacle. Dozens more of them flicked in and out of the water all around the creature, a collar of appendages that must have held the pulsating mass afloat.

Soon he stopped tumbling and remained flat, stomach down, arms out in front of him, but his descent put him on a course toward the tumultuous water encircling the beast. That's when he saw its horrible mouth. He felt the presence of the Angel of Death then, but its touch wasn't cold or hard. Rather it applied a friendly pressure to his shoulder and seemed to whisper, "Is it such a bad way to go, Abel Sykes, being swallowed into a beast as impressive as this?"

But he was kidding himself. There was plenty of unpleasantness ahead if he continued toward the behemoth's maw, for its throat was studded with teeth designed to puncture and tear. Near its dead-gray lips, the teeth were far too large to be thought of as sharp or pointed, but they quickly diminished in size the deeper inside Abel's gaze wandered. Whatever the thing was, it was clear to him that it had but one sole purpose in life: to ingest as much living meat as it could before it died. The ravenous, lolling eyes, too accustomed to the sunless fathoms of the ocean's deepest pits, confirmed this. So did the hunger-driven agitation of the flexing rows of teeth.

But the leviathan had seen enough of the bright topside world, and down it plunged like a sinking continent. Abel was so close now he could smell the thing's breath, which was a rotten, fishy wind to be caught up in. Mercifully it twisted away from him as it dove, so he didn't have to stomach the offending air for long, but he was sucked into the quickening maelstrom of its wake. Even before he reached the water level, a kind of vacuum was at work on him, and now he, too, was in a mighty plunge for the ocean's bottom.

To the extent that Abel could hold a coherent thought together in the spiraling torrent that dragged him down, he assumed he was destined to drown at last. Yet the rushing tunnel ensconcing him showed no signs of narrowing, at least not enough to prevent something as tiny as a man from passing through. A more immediate danger than drowning, though, was the dizziness beginning to claim him as he tumbled away, glancing off the curved wall of the watery funnel and ricocheting back across, over and over, ever downward.

Whatever the real dangers to his person, Abel's mind soon focused on a single inescapable reality: it was getting dark. He'd never adored the warmth and brilliance of the sun more than now, when the prospect of its permanent withdrawal closed around his neck like a garrote. Still he crashed around and down, losing more light with each revolution of his body.

He was completely blind by the time the rushing water deposited him roughly on some kind of rock shelf. It took him several moments to realize he was no longer in the water but in some kind of grotto. How was it possible? How could there be an air pocket in the very ocean? Then he realized it was probably temporary, the result of the raging eddies left behind by the descending monster. Which meant it was only a matter of time before water refilled the cavern, drowning him after all and washing him out of existence. He could still hear the din of water being siphoned away, but it wasn't close—yet. Once he found the strength to lift his weary body from the stone floor, he got up on his knees and began feeling around with his cold, shivering hands, desperate to gauge the dimensions of his new habitat.

On his left he quickly encountered an edge and violently recoiled from the bottomless abyss he imagined extended from it, but in so doing, he backed into a wall, giving his head a good knock. Dear God, he thought, how confined am I? He soon had his answer. The ledge he occupied seemed to be roughly crescent shaped, extending no more than four feet ahead and eight across. Venturing to stand on wobbly legs, Abel reached as far up the wall as he could. He found no edge, not even a handhold. Abel Sykes had found his watery grave, and now he longed to return to the whaling life.

That was impossible, of course. There was no whaling life to return to, even if he were to risk a fatal case of caisson disease by finding his way to water—or waiting for it to find him—and letting himself shoot to the surface. His vessel sunk, her crew gone, he had no hope of existence beyond this underwater shelf.

Perhaps for the first time in his life he contemplated the connectedness of things. He was no student of metaphysics, but how could he not wonder if his ultimate fate was tied up in his own actions prior to the colossus's breach? Murder hadn't been on his mind when he fell asleep the previous night, or when he awoke in the morning. Suicide was another matter. That had been in the works for some time, as tends to be the case with those whose crimes are so numerous and dire that most of them defy the reach of memory. But he'd never understood the blackguards and miscreants who felt the need to take as many innocent lives as possible with them when they destroyed themselves. Why couldn't they just slice open their own throats and be done with it?

Well, Abel Sykes would now die the perfect hypocrite. He'd slaughtered an entire whaling crew with every intention of making himself the last victim, and now that death was an imminent certainty, he wanted life more than he could remember ever wanting anything before. To step once more onto dry land and take in the spiced air of autumn. To observe again the fashionable elite as they thronged the city streets at night—and maybe lighten their purses by a coin or two. To swell with the anticipation of future voyages and the profits they might bring. All of it was gone from him. In a sense, he was already dead. The rest was formality. Worst of all, he had absolutely no idea why he had done it. Some kind of cabin fever, he supposed.

Again, the feeling came over him that it hadn't needed to be this way, that the creature might not have come if Abel hadn't so recently left the good captain's quarters after separating his head from his neck with an axe. Hadn't laid the bloody implement against the doorframe before exiting the scene with such moral certitude. Hadn't prided himself on the mass murder so newly concluded. And maybe under those alternate circumstances that could never be, Abel Sykes would have found a reason to go on.

At least his situation could get no worse. Surely he'd arrived at the nadir of his existence. Death would come as a kind of release, a blessing even. He almost smiled in the dark.

Then the clicking began, as did the echoing trickle of water nearby. Something was climbing out of the pit, skittering up the rock face to the edge of Abel's roost. Faster now, and louder. *Tchck! TCHCK!! **TCHCK!!!*** Whatever it was, there was more than one. It wasn't the sound of their ascent that he was hearing, however. As they poured onto the ledge and over his body—dozens, at least, of the wretched stinging and gnashing things—he recognized the clicking noise as some sort of communication among their ranks. This was their call to feast, and Abel's only comfort was that he was spared the sight of whatever tore him open and gorged on his moist red insides in the dark—for he was spared no measure of agony or regret as he let fly a bone-rattling final scream.

SLIPKNOT

Sheriff Leroux leaned back on the hind legs of his wooden chair and brought his feet up to rest on the desk. The action kicked up a little cloud of dust from the planks of the floor. He surrounded the toothpick in his mouth with a thin smile. A little dust suited the place. His fingers drummed on a telegram as he stared at the noose that hung from a crooked nail on the wall. With his free hand he pushed his hat a bit farther up on his head, freeing several sweaty locks of black hair.

"Time to take you off sabbatical, old Slipknot. Your work's not done yet, by God." His voice was scratchy and carried the hint of a French accent from his Louisiana upbringing.

The door flew open and slammed against the wall. In ran Deputy Hapford. He stopped in front of the sheriff's desk, out of breath. Leroux didn't jump or shout but calmly brought one leg down, then the other, before scraping his chair closer to the desk.

"Who's on fire, Deputy?" he said. He took the toothpick from his mouth and rolled it back and forth between his thumb and middle finger for a moment before poking it back into his smirk.

"You must notta heard yet," the deputy said, still lacking breath. "They've caught themselves a suspect. An Etonville fella."

"A negro," Sheriff Leroux corrected.

Hapford smiled and removed his Stetson so he could play with its creases. "So you *have* heard," he said. "Sheesh, how'd you find out already?"

Leroux gestured to the telegram on his desk. "Sounds like a shut case."

Hapford glanced at the noose. The sheriff stood up and walked over to it.

"Something that pretty, and with that much history, ought to be hanging in a museum," Hapford said.

"That's not the kind of hanging she's accustomed to." Leroux turned to face his deputy. "And her career's not quite over."

* * *

Outside, the world was a bright, wavering mass of heat mirages. It was good to be out in the still Colorado air. Manning an empty jail made Leroux jittery. Someone wasn't working hard enough if there were jail cells sitting empty. That's how he viewed it. A lot of crime was being committed in those parts, plenty of unsavory behavior to keep every jail in five counties full to brimming with robbers, murderers ...

Rapists.

His eyes narrowed as he stepped off the boardwalk into the empty street that ran right through the middle of Arrowhead. Built up on an ecstatic binge of prostitution and gold fever, the town was now little more than a husk, waiting for a strong enough wind to come along and carry it away with the tumbleweeds.

"What did that city slicker call it?" Deputy Hapford asked.

Leroux looked back at the jailhouse entrance. Hapford leaned against the jamb. In the shade of the awning he was indistinct. Leroux squinted even more.

"The fella who was out here last fall," Hapford continued, "looking for a place to set up his printing press."

"Said it was a wraith town," Leroux replied.

"Yup, that's it. Wraith town. Not quite a ghost town, he

said, but working day and night to get there. Goddamn right."

The sheriff headed across to the saloon. The squawk of the batwing doors was the only sound in the place, other than the fall of his boots as he stepped up to the bar. No bartender in sight. He picked up a shot glass and knocked on the bar with it. "Curt!"

"Sheriff Leroux." It was the whisper of a snake.

He spun around to face the whisperer, his hand falling from instinct to the gun on his hip. In a dark corner, sitting beside a piano that looked to have a scar from every glass of beer that ever sailed across the room, was a small man with a very large black hat.

"Otto Schichter," Leroux said. "What cloud of stink did you float in on?"

"Oh, Henri. There's no cause for insults. I'm here on friendly business. Come, join me for a drink." He brought an empty tin mug to his lips and wiped invisible beer foam on his sleeve.

Leroux's skin crawled, but he joined the man.

"You suppose your barkeep is sleeping one off upstairs or what?" Otto said.

"Let's just have it," Leroux said. "What brings the law of Etonville all this way?" He pointed at Schichter. "And if you call me Henri again I'll break your fuckin' hands."

"My, such language. Is that what got you kicked out of the seminary?" Otto laughed himself breathless, though Leroux just sat there, still as the air itself, no more than a razor grin on his face. Otto took another drink of nothing before going on. "Listen—Sheriff Leroux—I'd guess you're probably entertaining thoughts of dragging that rope of yours across county lines, maybe stirring up more trouble in my humble burg than need be the case."

Leroux ground a spur into the floor, slowly rolling it back and forth. He liked the rough sound of it, like knuckles cracking. "Just doing my part to see that justice is served, Otto. Don't see the harm in that."

"Shit, Leroux. How many men have swung from that loop? Fifty? More? For God's sake, the law's supposed to stomp on trouble wherever it finds some. Ain't supposed to go looking for it. Or worse, starting it."

"More than a hundred."

"Pardon?"

"That's how many have choked out their last while dancing at the end of Slipknot. You can call them men if you like, but sixty or more was niggers. A good two dozen was redskins. Ain't a decent one among them, and if I can spread that gospel as easy as making Slipknot available for the occasional hanging, then I'm doin' the service of the Lord."

"Some don't see it that way. Word's starting to spread that maybe you're growing a little loose in the head. People are looking for ways to make peace. They want solutions, not more problems. The kind of hate you stir up with that damn—"

Leroux shot to his feet, knocking his chair over in the process. "The hate that *I* stir? I guess the woman beaters and cold-blooded killers of the world ought to just be left alone, free to spread *their* fear and *their* hate. Who do you think you are, anyway, coming into my town with your smug ideas about justice?"

"Okay, now settle down. I guess I didn't come here expecting to change your mind about anything." Otto rose now, too. "But give *this* some thought: that haunted noose you set so much store by, its history goes before you. You can't take that blood-stained piece of rope anywhere in three counties—hell, anywhere in eastern Colorado—and find a lawman or rancher who doesn't know something about its past. Ownership of such a thing as that comes with some responsibility. People are in awe of the rope, not the man who ties it to the tree."

It was no use dignifying the man's lecture with a response, so Sheriff Leroux simply waited for Otto Schichter to get up with a touch of his hat brim and walk through the doors and out of sight.

"That you, Sheriff?"

Leroux looked up to the balcony, where a fat, hairy man

had both hands on the railing and was staring down at him. The man wore nothing but cowboy boots and a grimy pair of dungarees, suspenders hanging limply at his sides. He rubbed his ample belly with one hand.

"There you are, Curt. Would have bought a drink from you five minutes ago."

He was going to ask the bartender what had him in bed at that hour, but it became clear when a tall, full-figured woman with a mass of red hair that spread like a flame from her halo to her hips joined Curt at the railing. Her breasts bulged from a partially buttoned nightgown that wasn't meant to cover much to begin with.

"Hi, Sheriff," she said, smiling and waving with her fingers.

Leroux didn't respond as he made for the exit.

The heat outside calmed him instantly. He did his best thinking in the heat. Standing in the middle of the street, trying to decide where to take himself, he guessed it to be the hottest day of the summer so far. He smiled thinly and gave a lazy salute to the sun as he made off to the west.

He felt something that was unfamiliar at first as he sauntered across town. Looking down he saw that he'd sprung a bastard of a hard-on and was reminded of his revulsion toward the sex act. He punched it with his fist. Again, harder this time. Finally it went soft and he was master of his thoughts once more.

* * *

The wait felt long, but finally the day came for justice to be served in Etonville. Sheriff Leroux and Deputy Hapford rode side by side at a leisurely pace through the hilly grasslands that lay between Arrowhead and Etonville. Slipknot hung from the sheriff's saddle horn and slapped against his steed's sweat-lathered neck. Leroux might have made the whole trip in silence, but his deputy was a nervous man by nature, and on a ride of any duration he insisted on chattering.

At the outskirts of Etonville a small crowd was gathered. Men, women, and children stood blocking the road.

"Word does travel, don't it?" said Hapford.

That haunted noose you set so much store by, its history goes before you.

Leroux pulled his horse to a stop only when he was almost upon the crowd of gawkers. He'd half expected them to part at the last second and let him through, but they didn't budge.

A plump woman in country dress stepped right up alongside him and broke the ice.

"We know who you are—and why you've come. Well, Etonville can handle its own problems just fine without any help from you, or that damned relic you carry around like a good-luck charm." She eyed the noose but only for an instant. "So why don't you just turn yourselves around and stick to defending your own town."

"Ma'am ..." Leroux tipped his hat and leaned toward her in his saddle. "You can't be the woman who was forced into beastly acts with a darkie, seein' as how she took her own life and all."

"No, sir. But—"

"So I have no words for you, and you have no authority over me." He spurred his horse and let out a *hyah!*, and this time the crowd did part to let him and his deputy pass.

As the two of them rode to the center of town, where the hanging tree sat hunched over the barren ground beneath it like a beaten hostage, Otto Schichter emerged from a tiny jailhouse across the way. He met them in the street.

"I guess you already know how welcome you are here," Otto said, looking up from beneath the brim of his enormous hat.

"I'm not here to gain friends," Leroux said.

"No. Well, I'm sure there's little danger of that. I trust Eva Tucker had a word or two for you."

Leroux jumped down from his horse and led it by the

reins. "I'm just going to hitch my ride outside the jail there and then do what needs doin' and go home."

"Dammit, Leroux. We've got a noose in this town, you know. We've also got a judge, and he didn't come to the decision of hanging lightly. To be honest, there's some folks hereabouts who think there's maybe a question or two about this young man's guilt."

"And there's at least one citizen hereabouts who's convinced enough that he saw fit to send me a telegram." Leroux pushed past Otto and tied up his horse.

Hapford did the same.

Otto called after the two of them, "Isn't it enough for you that he's getting a public hanging?"

"Sheriff Schichter," Hapford said, "let him do this and we'll be on our way. What's it to you if this damn ape swings from one rope or another?"

"The question is," Otto shot back, "what's it to *him*?" He stabbed his thumb in Leroux's direction.

Leroux ignored their exchange and was pulling Slipknot down from its perch when something caught his eye. He looked over at the barred window of the jail. At first all he saw were two black fists, each wrapped around an iron bar, but a face soon came into focus. A pair of tired eyes stared out at him from the black of that face and the almost inseparable black of the cell.

"That the one?" he asked Otto.

"Now Leroux, don't go doing something you'll regret later."

"You the one raped that poor woman?" He turned his attention back to the prisoner. "You the one broke into her house while her husband was out huntin' and put your dirty black hands all over her?"

The man behind the bars just stared back with those worn-out, pitiable eyes.

"Yeah," Leroux went on, "I don't really care to hear anything you'd have to say anyway." He went around the hitching post and, taking a step forward, let a wad of spit fly into the captive's face.

The man's eyes closed as the phlegmy mass caught his cheek, but when his eyes flashed open a second later his gaze was as direct as before. Without pause he launched his own ball of saliva at Sheriff Leroux's face. It was a direct hit.

Leroux choked back anger. He wasn't about to let a hell-bound nigger make a fool of him.

"Well," he said, "I guess we can both wipe our faces off. The difference is, if someone comes along an hour from now and spits in *my* face again, I'll be able to wipe that off too, whereas you'll be hanging by your neck from that tree back there." For added emphasis he brought Slipknot up several inches and gave it a shake.

A little while later, after one of the local boys had set up a ladder under the hanging tree, Sheriff Leroux stood on the top rung but one, wrapping his pride and joy around a limb that might have been designed for lynching. His movements were oddly carefree, as if he were stringing decorations for a harvest dance instead of setting the noose that would end a man's life.

"Keep the ladder steady now," he called down to Hapford, who held on with both hands.

"Ain't goin' nowhere," Hapford said back.

A wind came on and sent a chill up and down Leroux's back. Even though it was shaping up to be a scorcher, the mid-morning breeze cooled the flesh of his face and arms.

"All right, I'm coming down."

The Etonville welcoming committee was arranging itself around the execution site. Some others who hadn't been there to meet Leroux and Hapford at the edge of town were also converging on the spot. A few looked hungry for blood, but Leroux figured most were just curious.

"So," he said to his deputy, "I'll see you back in town?"

"Yup, I'll sign as a witness and bring Slipknot back with me. Don't you worry none."

"Much obliged."

"Yeah, me too."

Leroux touched his hat and went for his horse. He didn't say a parting word to anyone, just rode away from the hanging tree, away from the jailhouse and Otto Schichter's ward, away from Etonville itself. He hadn't gone far, however, before he heard a voice call to him from the brush at the side of the trail leading out of town.

"Mister Sheriff?"

He pulled his horse to a stop with a *whoa* and a quick tug of the reins. It was hard to tell exactly where the voice had come from, so he twisted his neck every which way, waiting for the speaker to say something else. Finally a little black boy emerged from off to his right.

"Was that you called out to me?" Leroux said.

The boy nodded, but the rest of his body was as firmly planted as a fence post, his hands clasped together at his waist.

"Well, what could an ornery little pickaninny like you want with me?"

"You the man who brings the hanging rope with you wherever you go, aintcha?"

"Where there's cause for it, yes. What's it to you?"

"Why ain't you sticking around for the show? You go to all that trouble to make sure a man gets hung proper and you don't even stay to see him off?"

Leroux let out a little laugh. "I never watch, son. I don't have the stomach for violence."

"That's my pop they's planning to hang today. No one else will listen to me, Mister Sheriff, and I don't suppose you'll be any different, but I gots to tell you, my pop is innocent. I was with him the whole time Mrs. Danvers was being attacked."

Leroux got down off his horse and walked it over to where the boy stood. He stared down into his frightened eyes.

"Boy, let me tell you something about life. There's the truth, and then there's the *truth*. I'll tell you the real truth, if that's what you want to know. And you can sing it to every Mary, Dick, and Sue in Etonville for all I care. Ain't one of 'em will believe you.

"I've got a deputy by the name of Hapford. Most people think he's a pretty decent man. A little light upstairs maybe, but good hearted. Well, their opinion of him would probably change quite a bit if they were to learn he has a little trouble keeping his dick in his pants. Not the kind of thing I usually condone, mind you, but a sheriff needs his deputy, and Hapford's as good at his job as I need him to be. So once in a while he stirs up a little trouble and I do my best to cover it up for him. Well, this time he stirred up a heap of trouble. And once again I'm covering it up for him. He owes me for this one, by God."

"You'd let my pop hang just so your deputy don't get found out?" Tears welled up in the boy's eyes.

"Son, I'd let your pop hang for spitting tobacco out the wrong side of his mouth. One day you'll see how things are around here." He mounted his horse again before finishing. "If you're smart, you'll move somewhere else altogether. If you're dumb, you'll stay here and wind up like your pop."

He rode off and left the boy in a plume of dust.

* * *

The boy stood there like that for a few seconds, trying to take in the man's words and avoid a crying fit. He'd been brought up to respect the law, but the injustice that was unfolding against his father had him questioning a whole lot of things.

"You can come out now," he said at last, his voice shaky.

From the vicinity where he had appeared came a large black woman and, behind her, Otto Schichter. The woman rushed at the boy and folded him up in her arms.

"Oh, Teddy!" she cried. "Well done, Teddy."

Schichter leaned back with his hands on his hips and flashed a smile almost as broad as his hat. "Yes sir. That was some fine questioning you done. What do you say we head on back to town and prevent a hanging?" Then, to the woman, "Might have to send Sheriff Leroux another telegram, too, inform him that his deputy's in good hands."

He led the way back into Etonville, and the boy and his mother followed close behind.

By the time they reached the town square, the accused was already seated atop Hapford's mount, Slipknot snug around his sweat-slicked neck. The ladder had been set aside, and Hapford stood nearby, arms crossed, staring up at the man.

"Hapford!" Otto hollered, quickening his pace and leaving the boy and his mother behind. "I believe we have some talking to do before there's any hanging in this town."

Hapford shot him a startled look, and without hesitating he slapped the horse's rump, sending the animal tearing off without a rider. Its gallop slowed to a trot before long, and soon it resorted to stamping lazy circles in the dusty road and whinnying as if confused.

But no one's attention was on the horse for long, because it turned out death wasn't as clean a business as many of the townsfolk had hoped. The supposedly executed man swung limp and motionless for several moments, but then he started to twitch and writhe. His body became a wave of jittery movements, arms and legs flailing in the late-morning sun. The crowd was still and aghast, and when his eyes flared open, red and wild with anger, everyone took a collective step backward and sucked in a breath of air.

Everyone, that is, except for Deputy Hapford. He was too busy running, dropping his hat, stopping to pick it up, mounting his horse, and galloping away to be a part of the witnessing. He could be heard calling to Sheriff Leroux all the way out of town.

* * *

Teddy stepped away from the group as his father gripped the rope above him with both hands and hauled himself up enough to begin chewing through the fibers.

"Pop?"

The man groaned in response, his teeth at work on the rope.

The boy's mother came to his side and laid a hand on his shoulder. He looked up and saw tears cutting through the dust on her face.

"Theodore," she said. "I don't think that's your daddy anymore."

That was all it took to scatter the onlookers, who trailed shouts of "Spirit!" and "Devil!" and "Ghoul!"

The man bit through the last strands of rope and fell to the earth with a grunt. He landed in a crouch and slowly uncoiled himself. Something like a smile stretched across his face as he pulled the noose over his head and let it fall to the dirt. Those red, gleaming eyes were once more on the boy, but mercifully the father-thing turned toward the jailhouse and tramped in that direction, its movements uncoordinated and labored. The boy's mother tried to hold him tight, but he had to follow, had to know.

Rounding the corner of the small building, the father-thing disappeared from sight. Teddy raced across the square in pursuit. Around back of the jailhouse, he watched it hunker down and start clawing at the earth, sending little clods of dirt up into the air. After many minutes of this, it stopped cold. It had found something.

Teddy circled around to get a better view and saw that his father was engaged in a struggle with another thing. In the father-thing's hand was the hand of someone long buried. Soon the arm came free, then the shoulder, and finally, sending up several clumps of dirt, the head. Its jawbone ground back and forth, and its dead lips peeled away from the few rotten teeth that remained in its horrible mouth. Teddy heard it mutter something, this monstrosity that now used its other arm to deliver itself from the hole. The father-thing stepped away and let the other come on its own. The ground all around the hole began to break apart, and the two of them helped more of their kind come free. Hands shot up out of the earth, followed by heads that groaned with the obvious pain of being resurrected. Soon the plot of dry earth behind the jail was teeming with the dead come back to life. There was purpose in this, Teddy sensed. They were being called.

He crouched in the rear entryway until the last of them was out of sight around the corner. Then he followed. They traipsed to the main road out of town and lumbered off in the direction of Arrowhead. Without turning his gaze from the awful sight of their exodus, he noticed that Otto Schichter was approaching him with some haste.

"Son?" Schichter said.

Teddy only swung his head slowly from side to side.

"Son, are you all right?"

"I think so."

"Good. I suppose it will take a while to sink in, what we just seen, but if you're unharmed, that's a start."

"What did Sheriff Leroux have against my pop?"

The things from behind the jail were almost out of sight over the crest of a hill. Dust swirled in their wake.

"Well, that's difficult to answer. Men sometimes get filled up with meanness at an early age. Some can get rid of it later in life. Others can't. I've known Leroux a long stretch of years, and in all that time I've never seen him commit a single act of kindness. I don't think simple human decency has anything to do with why he's a lawman. And I don't guess it helped matters any when his wife ran off with a colored fellow."

"The dead folk who crawled out of the ground just now are going after him, ain't they? They's all been hung by the sheriff's noose, I'll bet."

Otto placed a hand on Teddy's shoulder. "Son, if that's the case, there could be things like that coming back to life for miles around, looking for retribution. Our little potter's field isn't the only place where Leroux's handiwork's been buried over the years."

Teddy looked up and smiled at the man, comforted by the

shade from the brim of his hat. "Mr. Schichter, that sounds all right to me."

Schichter let out a laugh and moved his hand around to Teddy's back as he guided him away. "You know, it don't sound half bad to me, neither. Even better if Deputy Hapford is to their taste as well. Now let's go see how your mama's holding up, shall we?"

She sat under the gently swinging rope, turning the severed loop in her palsied hands. The way her dress spread out around her, it was almost like she was melting from grief. She looked up and wailed as Teddy and Otto came to a halt beside her.

"Mrs. Jamhorn," Otto said. "I know it ain't much, but I think some sort of justice is being served here today. We've got to believe that."

"Did you see what my husband turned into?" she sobbed.

"Yes I did, and I learned a long time ago that the Lord's works are as mysterious as they are good. You believe that, don't you?"

She nodded, casting her eyes downward.

"Good, because you've got a boy here that you've got to help turn into a good strong man."

"Mama," said Teddy, taking Slipknot from her and holding it at his side, "Let's get you home. You need rest."

She went with him reluctantly, and nothing further was said as she and her son walked home arm in arm, leaving the good sheriff to work up the lies he'd have to tell for years to come about what had taken place. Teddy didn't envy him the task. But then, Teddy had his own challenges ahead of him. His mother would need him at least as much as he needed her in coming days, and there was no guarantee that they'd ever really recover from their loss. That was the way of the world, and if it wasn't exactly fair, young Theodore Jamhorn thought, it might still be right somehow. Maybe that's what Sheriff Schichter had meant about justice. At any rate, Teddy was in no position to question the authority of God's will. Who was, after all?

HOMING

The paint had flowered away from the wall beneath his bedroom window. Most would have assumed that the area, no more than ten inches wide, had been that way for a long time and they were only now noticing it. Not Jimbo. His first thought was that the flaw had appeared earlier in the night while he slept, or maybe right before his very eyes as he sat there on the edge of the bed, staring at the wall in his candy-striped pajama pants, the glow of a streetlight through his window the only source of illumination.

The bare spot bore the shape of an inverted heart, which bothered him, so he reached forward, intending to worry a dirty-pink curl of paint away from the wall and change the shape. But there was something else about the blank area. His hand stopped cold in midair. His bare toes drummed silently, nervously, on the hardwood floor, and he leaned in for a better look. There was movement within the heart. A universe existed there, and it smelled like an ocean on fire.

Never having loved, he touched the living blemish with some hope. Time accelerated, drawing him into the hole with awful, shrinking fury. It felt like going home.

His neighbors might have understood the troubling shriek that echoed through the run-down apartment building if they'd watched him depart this world, leaving his skin and bones behind in a slick red pile, along with his candy-striped pajama pants.

NOT FOR ALL TO SEE

Ordinarily, nothing short of a fire drill or a thunderclap would have drawn Jennifer Higashi's attention away from her work, but this afternoon a seagull landing on the windowsill of her office was enough. Some Seattleites considered them a nuisance, but Jennifer enjoyed the birds, finding their flight elegant, their demeanor affable, and their design nearly perfect. However, watching the gull turn its head this way and that to get as complete a view of its surroundings as possible conjured up a distant memory of her father sitting her down at a favorite spot in Volunteer Park to disclose a troubling family secret. He was a huge fan of Burt Lancaster's movies, especially *The Bird Man of Alcatraz*. Her brain made strange connections like that sometimes.

There was something false about the film, in Jennifer's view, even though it was based on a true story. She had a hard time believing that a prisoner could feel anything but jealousy toward a bird. What sight could be more heartbreaking to an incarcerated man than that of a bird flying freely in and out of the prison yard? Wouldn't it be a deeply sardonic thing to endure? A matter of perspective, she supposed.

"Noodle-san," her father had said in his deeply accented English that day at Volunteer Park, "I must tell you something it will not be easy for you to hear, but it is also not easy for me to say. This is a difficult day for us both."

"What do you mean, Papa-san?" she'd asked, looking up into his eyes as they sat on a bench facing west toward the Space

Needle.

"I mean that you are almost a woman now, and that means more for you than it does for other girls. It means the way you see the world is about to change."

He'd been balling up his flat cap as he spoke, and she'd wondered if it would ever be wearable again. Then, gazing silently out across the park at the glittering water beyond the Needle, she'd listened to the rest of what her father had to say.

Sitting in her Pioneer Square office, she watched the seagull take several graceful steps along the casement and thumbed through the worries that had been planted in her mind fifteen or so years before. There would come a moment in her life, her father had said, when she would see a being that other people *do* not—*can*not—see. The ability ran in her blood, passed down through so many generations that no one knew if it had been meant as a blessing or a curse originally—or, in fact, how the weird talent had come to the House of Higashi in the first place.

Whether blessing or curse, tradition had a role to play as well. For instance, it was forbidden to discuss the object of her sightings with another living soul, even within the family. As a result, she had no idea what to expect, no comparison to things her father or brother may have witnessed with their third eyes, as it were. She'd spent years worrying that the effect on her might end up being like schizophrenia, leaving her disoriented and afraid, maybe even suicidal.

The gull took to the sky, and Jennifer felt her shoulders relax as she watched it seek out a thermal and then glide off in the direction of King Street Station.

That's when she noticed something strange.

A figure clung to the side of the station's clock tower, beneath the balcony parapet by five or ten feet but still at least seventy or eighty feet from the ground. Was it a man? How could a human have made it up the tower? She got up and went to the window for a closer look.

Is this why the seagull captured my attention, because subcon-

sciously I was picking up on this figure in the distance?

Not a man. It couldn't have been, unless men had started growing thick fur and developing the ability to scale walls with reptile ease.

Her desk phone rang, but she waited to uncross her arms and answer it until the figure had reached the balcony and slipped inside the tower through a slight sash window, which it then slammed shut.

She picked up the phone. "Hello, Jennifer speaking."

"Jennifer Higashi?"

She sighed. Sometimes her boyfriend's sense of humor was a welcome diversion. It ranked high among the things she found attractive about him. But this wasn't the day for one of his routines.

"The voice is very convincing," she said, "but I really—"

"I won't be back-burnered again, Ms. Higashi. You promised a delivery date of a week ago. I want that app in my pocket. Do you understand?"

"Nobody does business like that. Jesus, you've been laid off too long."

"Oh, come on." He relaxed into his normal voice. "Are you telling me you never get a call from a bloviating client?"

"I write apps for local, county, and state government. There's not a lot of negotiating, to be honest."

"Not enough personal investment from clients who are living in a Marxist dreamland, eh?"

"Too busy with other things, in a lot of cases. Is there something you want, hon, or is this just a bug-the-shit-out-of-Jennifer call?"

"Okay, okay. I can take a hint. You're busy. Call me later?"

The question gave her a nervous feeling she couldn't have explained, because as crazy as it was, that damn thing in the clock tower had her worried—enough to wonder if she *would* call Dyson back. She rubbed the arm holding up the receiver.

"Yeah, I'll try. Otherwise, see you at home, okay?"

"Okay, fine. Bye." The disappointment in his voice was

crushing. Then he was gone.

* * *

The air coming off the water at her back was cool, but there was no wind or rain. A pleasant enough day for a stroll to get a better look at the tower, and maybe another sighting of the figure.

She got a few curious looks of her own as she stood on the sidewalk along the Amtrak parking lot, staring up at the balcony the figure had used to enter the tower. Her father's voice filled her head.

If it sees you, it will hunt you, and if it hunts you, it will not stop until it catches you. What it catches it kills.

Why couldn't she have been burdened with sightings of something so cute and harmless it made rabbits seem ugly and mean-spirited by comparison? That was probably her older brother Rickie's luck, while she was stuck with a wolf-lizard that could scale vertical faces without any gear.

It didn't appear to be interested in making another appearance from the balcony, so Jennifer made her way into the station. It would be hopeless to press the Amtrak staff for information about the tower, so instead of disrupting their work she escorted herself up a short flight of steps leading to what must have been an entrance to the tower stairs. There was no elevator. She remembered hearing that, and she had no intention of climbing ten flights. But if the mysterious figure was indeed the being she was fated to see because of her family curse, her job was as clearly defined as those of the union workers who marched throughout the station and manned the check-in counter. She at least had to try the door, maybe have a peek inside.

There is only one way to end the creature's pursuit, Noodle-san. You must blind it. Only then will you be safe.

As she reached for the doorknob, she was surprised to see

that her hand was trembling. The door was locked tight.

Probably for the best, she thought as she walked back down to the main lobby and toward the exit. What would it have looked like to this crowd of strangers if she'd engaged in battle with the figure—invisible to them—right there in the station? They would have dragged her away with a butterfly net. She'd have to think more seriously about such things going forward.

Besides, was she truly prepared to go up against this thing? Why tempt fate by seeking a confrontation? Then again, why put off the inevitable? It's not like she could easily change jobs and move out of the area. Even if she did, maybe the thing would show up wherever she was, now that she'd discovered it. Wasn't that part of the curse, too? That once you'd seen your being, fate would be sure to keep it in your way? She thought she remembered something to that effect.

Halfway back to her office she stopped, overcome with the chilling certainty that if she were to turn around, she'd see the figure loping out of the station, clearing the row of taxis in a powerful leap, and pursuing her with a slavering maw and clacking claws. The thought in her head, she had to know—and slowly turned to face the truth. The figure was nowhere to be seen.

Until she looked up. There it was, clambering over the parapet high up the tower and scuttling, nose down, toward street level. She couldn't remove her gaze, even as it stopped in its descent and brought its snout away from the bricks. In a moment it would be returning her stare, but she could not look away.

Did it smile as their eyes connected? From such a distance it was hard to be sure, but one thing was clear enough. When it resumed its descent, it moved at a faster clip than before.

Shit.

And she was off. Second Avenue was her only immediate option, and since turning south would take her in the direction of the football stadium and farther away from downtown, she opted for north, which would eventually open up onto the financial district. Not that a crowd would be of any help when she was being hunted by a creature only she could see, but the old instincts remained. She would welcome the bustle of downtown, if she got that far.

A block farther along, however, she remembered a tiny urban park she'd visited a few times with her niece. It featured a manmade waterfall and a patio with several outdoor tables. You entered through a decorative steel gateway that gave the impression of leaving the city behind. She and Stacy used to have picnics there. Stacy had thought it was a magical place. Now Jennifer hoped it was. She'd never outrun the figure, but maybe she could hide from it long enough to buy herself some time. The park was another block up on the left. She didn't want to risk looking back while running, but she doubted it could have caught up to her so quickly. As soon as the distinctive metalwork separating the park from the street came into view, she picked up her pace and darted inside.

Taking cover behind a feature meant to look like a monolithic stone column, Jennifer did her best to gauge how many seconds she had until the inevitable appearance of the figure. If it hadn't spotted her as she entered the park, surely it had the ability to sniff her out, or at least guess at her intentions. The length of her wait might give her an idea of whether or not she'd actually been witnessed coming in, whether the element of surprise was hers. If nothing else it gave her something to focus on other than the rising tide of panic in her chest.

The park had been empty when she barged in, but an African-American man now entered with his daughter, maybe seven or eight years old. Cute as a kitten.

Dammit.

She had tried to pry more details from her father, but he was only allowed to say so much, he always claimed. It was logical, however, that many an unexplained accident and mysterious disappearance must have been attributable to figures unseen by most. Figures like the one tracking her now.

Especially if families other than her own had similar curses laid against them. It was too much for her agitated brain, like contemplating the infinity of cosmic history. It was cooler in the park, partly because of the shade, partly because of the waterfall at the back. Jennifer shivered a little.

"Get the fuck out of here!" she whisper-yelled at the father without showing herself. *"Leave or I'll blow your fuckin' heads off!"*

The child wailed in response, and the father scooped her up to make a hasty exit. Even if the figure hadn't heard Jennifer's false threat, it might have seen the man and child fleeing the park and wondered what was going on inside. *So be it.*

The girl would know to fear people now, probably saw already that her father couldn't predict everything, though he had protected her from the perceived harm of a lunatic. Maybe worst of all was that either the girl or the dad—or both—wouldn't want to return to Waterfall Garden Park any time soon. Maybe they *never* would. But they would live. She may have given away her location to ensure their safety, but whatever came next, the man and the girl would likely survive.

What *did* come next was a sour puff of air that made her gag deeply. It was accompanied by a low grunt. Stepping into view around the edge of the column was the figure, and Jennifer's assessment that it was a cross between mammal and reptile couldn't have been more spot on. Its fur-clotted snout protruded like an alligator's, even though it walked on two legs. Otherwise its appearance was largely lupine: erect ears, muscular body, fur all over. Until the tail came into view. When the figure had been crawling around on the outside of the train station's clock tower, the tail had been obvious, but its magnitude had not been. Up close the tail was clearly a mechanism of balance and power. It tapered away from the hips instead of from a central tailbone, so it was incredibly wide and flat at the base. Unlike most mammalian tails, it hung all the way to the ground, where it trailed off still farther, hairless, like a rat's. The figure itself stood over seven feet tall.

Jennifer's entire body was soaked with sweat, despite the chill in the air. Blinding the figure had seemed like a remote possibility, but seeing it up close, its large head gliding from side to side in search of its prey, she didn't have an ounce of faith in anything. She could actually feel belief draining out of her. Belief in the possible and the impossible alike, the unlikely and the proven, the experienced and the dreamed. Belief that she in fact existed and was staring down this bizarre creature that no one else in the world could see. All of it was flooding out of her. If she didn't act soon, she'd lose her mind right along with her nerve.

The figure found the pond into which the twelve-foot-high waterfall ran, and here Jennifer got her first dash of hope since seeing it invade the small space—smaller than she'd remembered from trips with her niece. It appeared to be transfixed by its own reflection in the water. Thoughts about the figure's origins and the nature of its existence wanted to claim Jennifer's attention, but now wasn't the time. If she really was going to attempt something as foolish as blinding the hulking brute, the time was now, while it was busy falling in love with itself.

If she'd had the right kind of weapon—a claw hammer or a garden trowel, say—she might have considered a frontal attack. Armed only with her hands, that wasn't an option. She ran to the figure's hind quarters and scaled its broad frame until she was at its shoulders. Once in position she surprised herself by letting loose a warrior howl. A glimpse of wild terror in the figure's reflection threw off her momentum, though. This was a living thing she was attempting to maim. Even though it longed to do at least as much to her, the moment wasn't without poignancy.

Nor was her attack, though momentarily delayed, without effect. Reaching around the formidable skull, and using the reflection in the pond for help navigating its crevices and protuberances, she dug the index and middle fingers of each hand deep into the thing's eye sockets and tore the eyes wide open with an outward ripping action.

An agonized yowl reverberated through the space, and she wondered if anyone other than her could hear it, or if sounds made by the figure were for her ears only. Something to quiz her father about if she got the chance—this wasn't over yet.

It tried to shake her loose, but she had an arm wrapped tightly around its throat. She didn't remember doing this, and it proved to be a mistake, for the figure, thwarted in its first attempt to rid itself of the violent parasite on its back, lunged backward, slamming Jennifer into the same stone column she'd chosen for protection earlier. It peeled itself away and left her to fall to the ground and regain her wind. Its hands rushed to cover its dripping facial wounds, so Jennifer wasted no time crawling to the ledge that skirted the pond and hauling herself over it, into the water.

She was in bad shape—several broken bones at least, not to mention a dull ache at the back of her head—and knew the adrenaline coursing through her system wouldn't last forever. That's why she'd gone for the water. The figure might not think to grope for her in the pond, and she knew she couldn't outrun it on the streets, even blinded as it was. It would smell her, hear her, find her. She felt sure of it.

Her left knee bumped against a smooth rock. Pulling it free of the pond she could tell it was a good heft for throwing. Maybe she had that much strength left. Watching as the figure, still groaning and grasping at the holes where its eyes had been, turned in pointless circles, she chose her moment to hurl the rock over its head and out onto the sidewalk.

For a moment she didn't think it was going to work. The figure turned toward the exit at the sound of the stone rolling away, but then it seemed to grow preoccupied with its suffering once more. Eventually, however, it dragged itself to the edge of the park, paused to test its sightlessness against the warm late-afternoon sun, and lumbered out of sight, trailing an animal scent that called to mind pelts and caverns. A slightly foul but natural smell. Slightly more bearable than the stench of its breath.

The pond didn't seem deep enough to drown in, but to be sure, she draped herself over the ledge, her face maybe a foot away from the exposed aggregate of the patio floor. There she lay as consciousness slipped from her damaged body.

*　*　*

"Noodle-san."

Her father's voice? Where was she? Her eyes wanted to open. She could feel them fluttering. "Papa-san?"

"Noodle-san!"

He'd been crying. She could hear it in his voice, and now she noticed he was squeezing her hand.

"Am I..."

"Save your energy," he said. "You've been hurt, honey, and I want to ask you something."

She tried to smile.

"The circumstances ... How they found you, it was unusual. I need to know, was it ... Did you see the thing that only you can see?"

She nodded.

"And did it see you?"

Another nod.

He closed his eyes and a tear leaked out. She watched it roll down to the corner of his mouth.

"Did you ..."

"Blind it?" she whispered. "Yes."

"That's good. Very good. You're a brave girl."

"Papa-san, is this the hospital? How long will I be here? I know I broke some bones ..."

"Yes, you're pretty banged up."

She could tell he was holding back sobs. "What is it?" she asked, sitting up a little.

"Your head. It took a pretty severe blow."

"How severe?"

"I want to tell you something, Noodle-san, about the curse."

"Okay." She was nervous, but she let him continue.

"I never wanted you to know this, but it might bring you comfort. There is one way to lift the curse, child. If a seer is killed by the thing she sees, the curse is ended, never to be passed on to a Higashi again."

The fluorescents were making her a little dizzy. "But—"

"Please, let me finish." He sniffed. "I wanted you to know the danger posed by these creatures, so you'd appreciate the importance of not letting yours see you, and of blinding it if it did. But I didn't want you to launch into a suicide mission to end the curse."

"Why are you telling me this?"

A digital chirp started up from somewhere to her right.

"Mr. Higashi, you'll have to leave now." A woman's voice. The doctor? A nurse? "We have a limited window of time ..."

Jennifer couldn't make out the rest. Sounds began to swirl, and the fluorescents in the room dimmed and dimmed and dimmed, light escaping like steam through a vent somewhere. Blackness seeped in like floodwater to fill the void, the way tsunamis actually encroach, not how they're portrayed in movies. She scanned for a brightness in the distance, the kind of light she'd heard about on daytime talk shows, but there was none. Only the spreading, deepening, inexorable dark.

Here comes the greatest unknown. All alone, so cold and afraid. I don't want this. Rushing toward ugliness and chaos. No comfort, curse or no curse. Someone, help!

"Jennifer, I love you."

Dyson? Back there in the light with Papa-san. Their darkness will come, too, but this journey, now, is mine alone. A journey into horrible stillness.

I love you too.

FULFILLMENT

When I was a young boy, my grandfather laid a curse on me. I used to crawl up onto his lap and listen to him spin the most enthralling yarns. When Mother and Father were present, he narrated his made-up tales in a boisterous manner. He became each character and clutched me for a scare at all the right moments. He spoke in a loud, resonant voice that filled the house with that magic only storytelling can bring. But when my parents were gone or distracted, Granddad would lean in close and whisper, "One day the rats'll get you, boy. The rats is what'll bring an end to your days."

And so it has come to pass. The vermin have arrived in great numbers. At first I only heard them chewing beneath the floor, but they soon got into the walls and ceiling. Their scratching got so bad I went a week straight without sleep. Now they've got into my living space. Not all of them yet, but I've seen five or six racing along the floorboards, diving into shadows.

They eat dog shit, by the way. My Ginger had taken to loosing her bowels in the house before she passed, and sometimes I wouldn't get to it right away. One night I watched a couple members of the rat horde nibble away at a pile of her spoiling feces. That's the kind of creatures I'm dealing with here.

I finally caught one yesterday. I looked up from *Judge Judy*, and there he was, perched on the mantle, eyes gleaming red. I reached for a plastic grocery bag and rushed the cocky bastard.

He tried to get away but ran up against obstacles in both directions, got real scared and froze. I don't doubt he would have leaped for my face if I'd been a whit slower, but I got that sonofabitch trapped in the bag before you could say Jack Robinson.

It seemed the best thing to do was keep twisting the bag around on my way to the kitchen, so that's what I did. He still managed to bite me a good one through the thin white plastic, but that was his last great accomplishment before I flung his ass into the freezer and snapped the door shut. That's when I learned how much noise a pissed off rat can make. He slammed around in there for five solid minutes, squealing to raise the dead. But eventually the sub-zero chill must have slowed his scampering limbs, frozen his manic will—and eventually his heart. I can only imagine, for I haven't opened the freezer to observe the state of things.

I sit and I wait. I can hear their undulating tide beneath the floorboards, hungry for ingress. I've painted everything with peanut butter. They can't see for shit, but the faintest scent of peanut butter sends them into a crazed caloric lust. It's on the walls and ceiling, the furniture and window sills. Forty-eight jars of Peter Pan.

They will find the stuff all over me as well. My arms, legs, groin. All through my hair. The rats will eat well tonight, and I will be with my grandfather once more.

You were right, Granddad. You were right all along.

RIDLEY BICKETT'S TRAVELING PANOPLY

Nathan stood on the hill, looking down over the midway with the deepest longing he'd known since landing at the bottom of his life. Only because of the full moon could he make out the silvery ripple of red-and-white-striped canvas in the breeze, or the row of trucks and trailers in the distance. Two large tents claimed the grounds to the right. Rides and small game tents huddled to the left. Conifers rimmed the area, while poplars, maples, and dogwoods dared to inch in for a closer view. He drew a half empty bottle of bourbon from inside his worn, dirty suit jacket. June was an unpredictable month in western Washington, and when he woke up one recent morning on the courthouse steps to find the jacket lying next to him, he'd seen no reason to leave it for someone else. It had looked new then, maybe a gift from some caring soul who'd passed by in the night. Already it was little more than a rag, which suited him fine. He took a long swig and replaced the bottle.

Carnivals rarely came to Stutton County, so when they did they got a lot of attention. This one more than most. Ridley Bickett's Traveling Panoply billed itself as a return to the glory days of carnival freak shows. Nathan had been around long enough to know that it couldn't really be a throwback to the nineteenth-century horror shows that used to roll through the American landscape peddling cheap thrills to simple folk. There were laws, after all. Gone were the days of gathering up the crippled and the insane, pitching them into horse-drawn cages, and grooming them to be star attractions. Good riddance. God knew Nathan would have been a likely candidate for abduction back then. But part of him wanted to believe in Ridley Bickett's bold claim, wanted to see the world with a child's wonder again. He supposed that was why he'd climbed this damn hill in the middle of the night, to capture something lost so long ago that he could no longer be sure it ever existed.

A chill wind rolled up the hillside, teasing the grass and weeds to life. Nathan might have taken the change as a signal to turn back and find a quiet doorway in town to finish his bourbon in, but the flutter of something shiny nearby held him in place. A card or ticket, about the size of a dollar bill. He stooped over without bending his knees and almost fell victim to a dizzy spell, but he was used to his body's idiosyncrasies and knew he could outfox the condition by easing himself down onto his rump, which is exactly what he did.

He plucked the item from the weeds. *Admit Two: Unlimited Access*, it read in bold script. A pass, good for the entire week the carnival was in town. Some poor kid was bound to be missing it, this being only day two. It felt good in his hands, though, stiff and glossy. He didn't care for the clown face that leered at him from one corner, but still, the pass brought on a flood of memories from carnivals he'd sneaked into as a boy. The chorus of tinny midway music, the rich smells of popcorn and cotton candy. He was never able to afford such treats, but they held as high a position in his memories of boyhood as they did for any suburban brat with a fat weekly allowance, maybe higher.

"Sir?"

Nathan cranked his head around to see who'd spoken. A boy stood nearby, a little higher up the hill. More of a young man, really.

"You startled me, son. It's not every day I'm addressed so formally. What brings you out by yourself at such an hour?"

"You won't tell on me, will you?"

"I'll let you know if you're in danger of saying something I don't want to hear. How's that?"

The boy didn't look convinced, but it was clear he wanted to unburden himself of something.

"I'm planning on joining up." The boy nodded toward the tents below. He looked like he had more to say, but no words came. His hands were fists inside the pockets of his wind-breaker, and he shifted his weight from one foot to the other.

"Feels scary coming right out and saying it like that, I'll bet. What's your name, son?"

"Ben. But there's no use trying to talk me out of it, if that's what you're thinking."

"Ben, I'm Nathan. Tell me, does your father beat on you?"

"No."

"Your mother drink? Sleep around?"

"Uh-uh."

"They make sure you have food to eat and a roof above you, I suppose?"

"I guess."

"Then what the hell are you runnin' away from?"

Ben took several steps down the hill toward the carnival, leaving his back to Nathan.

"My sister. I broke the head off one of her dolls and she told me she'll kill me in my sleep with a knife."

"Jesus." It came out in a whisper.

"She's got it in her, too. I've caught her doing things, to animals."

Nathan pushed himself back up onto his feet and went to the boy, placing a limp hand on his shoulder. "Son, I've got something here you might be interested in." He held up the shiny pass. "Good for all the rides and exhibits you can stomach. Tell you what, you take it and come here every day as soon as the carnival opens. Stay till it shuts down at night. If you haven't had your fill of the carnie life by then, why, you can march your-self right up to the last barker on the midway and ask where to sign up for a job. Go on, take it."

But Ben didn't take it. His eyes and mouth widened. Wonder clouded his features, as if he suspected the ticket was some piece of magic. Nathan's unconventional manner could have reinforced such an impression. But all of that was easily ignored for a moment as Nathan pretended Ben's reaction only hinted at some deep feeling passing between two human beings, at a friendship being forged. He thought he'd wrung the last of the tears from his eyes long ago, but now he felt like crying. It was a beautiful feeling, and he hoped Ben took his time answering so the moment would last.

"You think they'd show us around, even after hours?" Ben asked.

"Us? You mean you want me to go with you?"

"Admit two, right? Unlimited access."

"There wouldn't be anything to take in this late, except maybe the freaks. How much are you willing to see?"

"What do you mean?"

Nathan started down the hill. "Freak shows can be unpleasant things, is all, even in daylight hours—even if they're being faked, which I expect will be the case with some of these."

Ben followed in silence and they soon stood on the dusty midway of a carnival ghost town. Nathan perceived an echo of calliope music between gusts of wind, but it was probably just his imagination.

"I'm game," said Ben.

"Fair enough."

* * *

The decision of where to begin and who to disturb was made for them when an old man wearing a white tank top tucked into gray sweatpants stepped out from between the large tents to the right of the midway.

"A boy and a beggar," the man said in a voice like stones being ground together. He rubbed one hand over the top of his bald head as he spoke.

Nathan and Ben looked at each other, surprised.

"It's usually one or the other, not both. How come you, then, to Ridley Bickett's house of wonders at this late hour?"

"How?" Nathan said. "We come curious." Was it the remnants of white greasepaint that streaked the other man's neck?

"And in peace," Ben added with several quick nods.

"All right, *why* have you come, if that syntax is more pleasing to your refined ears?"

"The pass," Ben whispered while delivering a nudge of the elbow to Nathan's side.

"Yes, yes, of course. We have a pass, you see." Nathan took a step toward the old man and handed him the colorful ticket.

The man's eyebrows slowly rose and fell. "You've come to look at the freaks? Not for work?"

"Sir," said Ben, "the truth is—"

"What the boy means," said Nathan, "is that the truth is what we're after."

"The carnival after midnight is a strange place to go looking for the truth. But that's not to say it can't be found. You two interest me some. The name's Lautrec."

"I'm Nathan. This is my friend Ben."

"You're a drunk, aren't you, Nathan? I can smell it on your breath. Never mind, we all have our weaknesses. This way, please."

He led them to the far end of the midway, to the largest tent of the carnival. There he pulled back a voluminous flap and ushered them inside with a dramatic sweep of his arm. Now Lautrec appeared to have white circles of paint around his eyes. Odd that Nathan hadn't noticed them before. He hesitated, but Ben darted right in, leaving the drunken beggar little choice but to follow. Not that it felt like he had a choice in any of this to begin with. It was as if the night, and whatever lay ahead, had been written into his destiny from the beginning of time.

❋ ❋ ❋

A crooked, twisting aisle unspooled between two rows of alternating viewing panes and crimson drapery for as far as Nathan could see by the dim, wavering candlelight of the tent's interior. Candles glowed from the tops of stands the height of a man, but beyond their slight comfort a dreadful darkness presided.

"You've come to look," Lautrec said, "but you will also see. Our day visitors are admitted to the smaller tent. That's where you'll find the goat with five legs, the creature with the wings of a bat and the body of a vulture. That sort of thing. All very amusing for the simpleminded, but we feel our night visitors deserve a bit more. Bear in mind, what you're about to witness comes with an obligation. You must act on the impulses these exhibits engender in you, take what you learn here out into the world and subvert the lunatic course your breed has chosen for itself. All who are willing to carry that mantle are welcome here. All others are trespassers and will be dealt with accordingly. Do you accept these terms?"

What was there to say other than yes? Of course, yes.

"Very well. Then let us begin." Lautrec waved a hand over something and there was light within the closest exhibit on their right. "We start with an old idea, but one that bears repeating. You see these children?"

Ben gasped and Nathan's knees threatened to give out. A boy, wan and stupid looking, gaped at them, scratching the rags he wore with nails like claws. Beside him slouched a girl, emaciated and filthy. Her lips peeled away from black teeth in an unsettling rictus. This one's gaze roved but paused on Ben and Nathan with each pass.

"Mother of Christ," Nathan muttered. "Who *are* they?"

"The boy is Ignorance. The girl is Want."

"Dickens?"

"Dickens."

"What are you both talking about?" Ben wanted to know.

"Characters from *A Christmas Carol*," Nathan explained. "Shown to Scrooge by the Ghost of Christmas Present."

"A troubling passage, lad," said Lautrec. "A very troubling passage. So troubling you'd think enough people would have taken the message by now. Not so, I'm afraid. Ignorance flourishes in the world. Want thrives. And so we continue Dickens's work."

"Where did you find such creatures?" Nathan asked.

"He hails from Jerusalem, the girl from Sudan. But they have countless brothers and sisters in every corner of the globe. Let's move on."

They passed several darkened exhibits before Lautrec illuminated one on the opposite side of the promenade with another wave of his hand. Tight red curls hugged his scalp now, and his cheeks appeared lightly rouged. Either a strange trick of the light was obscuring Nathan's perception of their guide, or the man's appearance was changing.

"I'm not sure I want to see more," said Ben, his voice trembling.

"You *shouldn't* want to. Not entirely. Come."

Something simian sat on a rock, staring but mute, its expression wise and sorrowful. A single phrase, repeated a thousand times, claimed every inch of the pinewood walls that enclosed the animal on three sides, scrawled in what appeared to be mud but might have been something else: *I WILL DIE!* Over and over, *I WILL DIE!*

"Charlie here comes with a cautionary footnote. Play God only if you're willing to stare down your own handiwork. What you're looking at is the offspring of a union between a male human and a female chimpanzee. He was conceived in Switzerland, and no artificial insemination was required. No Swiss entity is willing to own up to this abomination. Charlie is presumed to be the only non-human animal in existence with awareness of its own mortality. An unhappy fate for the stolid brute, I'm afraid."

They wound their way through the rest of the tent in a rough spiral that drew them inexorably toward the center. They passed by many darkened exhibits and paused briefly at others, but they lingered at the most poignant examples of man's errors. Lautrec relished the telling of his moral lessons and had an attentive audience in Nathan and Ben. When they reached the final stretch of horrors, Nathan noticed that one exhibit was already lit up.

"End of the line?" he said.

"In a manner of speaking, yes. Ben, why don't you have the first look at this one. It's something rather special."

Ben looked from Lautrec to Nathan and back again before moving in front of the final enclosure. He spun around as soon as he caught a glimpse inside. "I don't get it. What does this mean?" His voice brimmed with anger and fear.

Nathan stepped within view of the scene. A young girl paced as much as the chain allowed that ran from a collar at her neck to a thick staple on one wall. She held a small knife in one hand. "You know this girl?"

"It's my sister."

"That's right," said Lautrec. "You choose carefully when to tell the truth and when not to, it seems. You were also correct when you told your friend here that Amelia wants to kill you."

"Hey, what is this?"

"What you failed to reveal is that you've got it coming. Put a meat fork in her precious rabbit's neck, didn't you, boy? Oh, we have eyes and ears everywhere. Believe it. And you lied about your parents, too. Or have you forgotten how your mother used to make sure you were watching whenever she made out with strangers? Do you miss the regular beatings now that dear old Dad's fled the scene? Lickings he used to call them, I believe. Unfortunately, young man, none of this works in your favor. You don't get a free pass to painfully execute a defenseless animal just because your parents are worthless. It doesn't work that way."

Nathan sensed a rustling movement amid the dark drapery to the right of Amelia's cell. A disfigured monstrosity emerged—a man, presumably, but one who had suffered such horrible burns that his joints seemed fused tight, the way he ambled into view and took the boy by the shoulders. Ben put up a struggle and cursed a good deal, but his efforts were useless against this creature's stooped might and implacable will. It licked at the edges of its mouth before disappearing behind the drapes with its prey.

"Who in the—"

"That, Nathan, was Ridley Bickett. Lucky to be alive, too. He rushed into a burning house many years ago to save the children of the man who set the blaze. The incident left him scarred in more ways than one. But we can discuss that another time. First, your final lesson for tonight."

Lautrec pointed to the glass. Bickett finished chaining up Ben opposite Amelia and then retreated. She arced her little knife with great savagery in her brother's direction, but he remained out of reach, barely, already taunting her with barbs and gestures.

"There's no place for this kind of behavior in the world. They're not the product of shoddy parenting alone. They're the product of a disengaged society. We made them, yet we cannot tolerate their violent ways, their madness. These two cannot be unmade. It's too late for that. But they need not have counterparts in future generations. That's where you come in."

"Me?"

"You, Nathan. Go out among the world and teach what you've learned here."

"What *have* I learned?

"Why, that what we do matters. It all matters."

Nathan finally tore his gaze from the children, and before him stood a full-fledged clown, bedecked in an orange costume with white polka dots and ruffles at the cuffs and collar. Wooly red hair encompassed his head like backlighting from another world, and enormous shoes covered his feet. Through heavy layers of greasepaint, Lautrec smiled broadly. The smile turned to chuckling, which grew to deranged, mocking laughter.

The request made little sense to Nathan, but there was no way he was spending another minute in that tent with a deformed man, a sinister clown, and the countless captive atrocities that made the dark their home. Lautrec was letting him go, it seemed. That was good enough for him. He'd miss the boy. There was no sense lying to himself about that. But he still had a third of a bottle left in the pocket of his suit jacket. It wouldn't dull the pain of losing a friend so newly discovered, but it might curb the anger he felt toward himself for being taken in by a kid.

Outside, the cool night air carried the faint strains of calliope music—he swore it did—but at least it drowned out the hideous laughter that continued to peal from inside the tent, if not the questions and doubts that stormed through Nathan's head as he walked back to town in search of a place to bed down.

BREECH BABY

L u Ellen wondered if things would be any different after she was dead. Would these people still have dinner parties and not notice she was gone, the way they now failed to notice she was there? None of them knew she was scared to death over the pain in her belly. No one even knew it was there. Maybe it was a tumor and one day it would burst open and get into the works of every system in her body and she would lose the ability to function. Doris would still take delicate sips of her merlot. Lukas would push food around his plate with a knife before loading it onto his fork. Ham would bore the company with tales he thought were some of the greatest ever told but that were really just puffed-up scraps of wish fulfillment. Lu Ellen hated the lot of them and wished her cancer would explode right there in front of them all, if cancer it was. At the first quiver she'd yank her blouse from the waist of her slacks and expose the throbbing growth. That would be enough to get Doris barfing into the kale salad. Then, when the thing actually broke open and oozed its mutated contents onto the spotless white tablecloth ... Well, the room would erupt into chaos and Lu Ellen could die content.

But God was seldom so kind about these things. Mysterious ways and all that shit. She would have to wait this out, like the dinner party itself.

The question was, Why did she keep getting invited to these fucking things? And why did she keep showing up? They had to hate her every bit as much as she hated them. She supposed they were all sick in one way or another. Lukas was standing now, an idiot's smile on his dumb face. Who did he think he was fooling with his polyester get-up, the sleeves of his sport coat intentionally a little too short, his necktie bunched up above the neck of his vest, although he surely would have called the tie a cravat and the vest a waistcoat. Did he want everyone to think he was some kind of poet? Not an intellectual, surely!

"Okay, everyone," Lukas said. "I've got an announcement to make, and I want you all to be the first to hear it. You already know that Elizabeth and I have been pregnant for over seven months now, and, well ... there's something wrong."

Beth sat beside her husband, her face ashen. Surely he'd told her he was going to do this. No, of course he hadn't. Selfish dolts like Lukas Harrington always expected surprise announcements to be well received by all. Lu Ellen didn't include Beth in her feelings about the rest of the group, she realized. Beth was different. Maybe she had something to do with why Lu Ellen kept accepting invitations to these goddamn dinners.

"The doctors can't seem to agree on exactly what the problem is, but the child probably won't survive unless they open Beth up early. See, it's adhered to the wall of—"

"Jesus, Lukas," Doris said with a mouthful of half-chewed sourdough.

"Well, imagine how *we* feel about it. Anyway, it won't make it if we try to bring it to term, and Beth would be at a highly elevated risk for complications, even death, if we took it out now."

Lu Ellen rubbed her abdomen. *Come on ... Pop, you sonofabitch!*

"So what are you going to do?" Ham asked.

"They're trying to talk us into a chemical bath that would slough the child out through the uterus, piece by piece. It would be the safest course for Elizabeth."

"Oh God, I'm going to be sick," Doris said before covering her mouth with a burgundy napkin and burping a little.

Beth had stopped looking at anyone. Her head hung so low

that locks of hair almost dipped into her soup. She might have been crying, but her body was still, so she wasn't sobbing uncontrollably, which she would have been more than entitled to.

"But," Lukas went on without invitation, a false smile still draining all substance from his face, "I think I'm close to convincing Elizabeth that the proper thing to do is force the birth now and then put the child up for adoption."

He'd said it like he expected praise, maybe even applause, but Lu Ellen only snorted laughter and shook her head, stabbing distractedly at some peas on her plate.

"What, she decided she was cool with the risk to her own life?" Lu Ellen said, nodding at Beth. "Beth, are you really going to let this rim job speak on your behalf?"

Beth eyed her with only the slightest raising of her head and quickly cast her eyes downward again.

"Shit, you people are all fucked up. I'm not perfect, but Jesus Christ, I'm Tony Robbins compared to the rest of you. Why would you go through all this and then put the kid up for adoption?"

Ham piped up, "I don't think you need to be—"

"No, no," said Lukas. "It's a fair question, just a little clumsy. We think the hand of God is in this, frankly, that he wants us to give the gift of a son to a couple who can't conceive on their own."

"Bullshit," Lu Ellen said. "There's a chance it'll be born retarded if it survives, isn't that right? And you don't want it to look like you're aborting a child simply because you don't want a retard for a son. But you *don't* want a retard for a son, so you figure you'll pawn the thing off to someone else ... again, if it survives."

She could tell Lukas was weighing not only his response but the manner in which he should deliver it. His eyes darted left and right, as if he were a fish in the dark.

"That's good," he finally said. "I admire your gall. It inspires me."

"Good, I'm glad it doesn't gall you. What if Beth dies? Does that concern you at all?"

"Of course it does. I wouldn't have mentioned the possibility if it didn't. But if we go with the chem—"

"Fine, I'll take you at your word. It's a risk you're willing to take."

"Yes."

"Beth, is it a risk *you're* willing to take?"

Beth lifted her head, and for a moment she looked more like a queen than the bullied waif she was. Pushing herself back a little from the table with both hands, she jutted her chin and stared defiantly at Lu Ellen, whose skin crawled with anticipation, for it felt as though Beth was about to say something momentous, possibly for the first time in her lonely life. But she said nothing. She stood, and the illusion shattered. The waif was back, and it cupped its hands to its face and ran from the room trailing quiet sobs.

"That's a lot of interesting talk coming from an orphan shit like you," Lukas said, spraying spittle across the table. A nervous smile played across his drooping lips. His cheeks reddened.

Lu Ellen could have come up with no better example of why she hated the man than this childish and misguided display. His timing was good. She had left herself wide open to the jab, and Lukas lunged. But the remark was an over-step, chosen for its guaranteed shock value more than its appropriateness to the situation. It betrayed a lack of confidence that Lukas should have found embarrassing, but of course he didn't. He was a stranger to all manner of humility.

"You're proud of that one, aren't you," Lu Ellen said. "It shows all over your jowly face. You're pleased with yourself for reminding everyone that I hate being called an orphan, because I'm not one."

"Adopted," Lukas said as he brushed at his thin mustache with two fingers. "Same thing."

Now everyone could plainly see what Lu Ellen had been the first to notice: Lukas had no idea where to draw the line, and he was an utter hypocrite.

"I should kill you," said Lu Ellen, calmly but with meaning.

"Oh, now, Lu," said Doris.

"No, really." She turned her attention to Doris. "For the depth of his stupidity I should scramble across this over-priced spread and tear his fucking eyes out. Who would care?" She looked back at Lukas. "Hmm? Would anyone in this accursed world shed a tear?"

The ensuing silence wasn't broken by an announcement from Ham that he really ought to be getting home to tend to his cats. It wasn't Doris observing that the hour was getting late, or even Beth returning with a contrite explanation for her sudden departure. It was Lukas who shattered the stillness, and he did so with a single syllable.

"No."

It was uttered with such certainty, such sincerity, that the room had little choice but to fall back into uneasy silence. Lukas sat down as Lu Ellen sprang to her feet.

Pain unlike anything she'd ever endured clamped around her abdomen. She started to bow over but the movement only made it worse, so she straightened herself and pressed both hands into the center of the pain. She could feel sweat beading all over her forehead and cheeks, then running down her chin and neck. Her skin felt hot. She pressed her eyes closed with so much force that she saw stars shooting this way and that.

"Jesus, Lu? Are you all right?" It was Doris.

Lu Ellen was incapable of speech. Something inside her fell, and the pain followed it. *Jesus Christ!* Wetness at her thighs, too much to be sweat. What, then? Blood? No, too much to be that as well. She'd be passing out by now if it was blood.

A surging pressure erupted in the region of her uterus. She desperately needed to lie down but knew she wouldn't make it to the floor without injuring herself further. The table was the only solution. Without bothering to clear a space, she slid herself to the middle and worked savagely to undo the belt at her waist. Then the button and zipper. Anything to relieve the pressure. In a clumsy display, she tore the pants from her legs and flung them aside, nailing Lukas in the face without even trying.

Finally she was able to let out a scream, but it was swallowed by the din of the other dinner guests, for they had dissolved into a state of panic. Her eyes flashed open. They were all staring and pointing at the area between her legs. She felt something there herself, something moving her underwear aside from within her vagina, very gently. Then, a tug, and the panties were ripped from her body, drawing blood where they friction-burned along her waistline. She grunted through clenched teeth. Whatever was inside her now had the egress it obviously sought, and it proceeded with the same gentle confidence of its initial toying. But this time it wasn't just fidgeting. It was on the move.

First, one slender black appendage rose into view from between her legs, crooked and spindly. Then a second, hairier than the first, emerged from her birth canal. They rotated and reached, as if testing whether the air was safe to breathe. Whatever they were attached to wanted out and began to push ... hard.

The others had stopped yelling but Lu Ellen took up the refrain. The pain was excruciating as something far too big for her to bring into the world forced its way nonetheless into existence. Two more insectile legs popped out but simply draped themselves over her thighs. The last four came fanning out above her stomach before falling across her midsection and taking hold. The thing was using its extremities to draw itself out of her.

In one final thrust, it burst free with a sloppy, wet sound, and Lu Ellen heard one of the party drop to the floor. Doris fainting, at a guess. Lu Ellen was very close to unconsciousness herself. But she had to see what she had birthed. She hitched herself up on one elbow, then the other. The black jointed appendages atop her began to arc, pulling the skin of her belly together as the gigantic head of an insane, curious spider came into view.

The thing quickly released its hold on her flesh and skittered over her leg onto the table. It seemed to assess the scene, its eyes searching the gaping faces of everyone in the room. Afterbirth clung to the arachnoid hairs that mantled its bulbous form.

Lukas was the first to run, and like that, the spider's decision was made for it. With a powerful leap it launched itself over the nearest chair back and dropped to the floor with a thud. Without so much as a beat, it was in pursuit.

Lu Ellen turned away smiling, the music of Lukas's horrified shrieks a lullaby that carried her out of this world and away from her last supper with these people, absolving her of the burden of explaining a most troubling delivery, and the recent nightmare she now believed had been much more than a dream.

THE PATIENCE OF ADAM

"**W**ould it kill you to spend some time with the child?" Bertram asked. "Maybe rock him once in a while?"

Whenever he held Adam, playing with his feet or feeding him, Eudora could barely stand to be in the same room. Now, in fact, she was only passing through to get more tea from the kitchen. Then it would be back to her sewing room, where she'd lose herself for hours in the threads of one project or another.

Bertram looked surprised when she stopped to answer his question. "Kill me? Oh no. If it were that simple I'd have patty-caked my way out of this sorry affair long ago."

"So much anger for an old woman," Bertram said as she whirled into the kitchen.

When she returned, he was smiling down at Adam, who greeted the look with his usual inquisitive stare.

"You're Granddad's precious angel, aren't you?" He tickled the boy's fat neck.

"I need to get away from this place, Bertram. I can't stand it anymore. We never see anyone. We never go out. All you do is dote on that damn boy, day in and day out."

"We're in our seventies, Dora. Where do we need to be running off to? It's peaceful here."

The child was looking at her, daring her to broach the subject that sat in her throat like a souring egg.

"Have you given any thought to the boy's future?" she asked.

Bertram cocked his head and she knew he was listening to the whisper of a quaking aspen through the nearby open window as a breeze pressed against the house.

"He doesn't belong with us anymore. Soon we'll be too old to care for him. What then? I know you don't like talking about it, but we must."

"What can we do?" He gazed out the window, Adam sitting unnaturally still on his lap. "Adoption's out of the question. You know that. They'd want to check on things."

"Yes, of course we can't put him up for adoption."

"Where does that leave us? Our families? Old friends? They all think he died years ago."

She took a step closer. "Now you've touched upon it, Bertram."

"Touched upon what?"

"The solution."

Adam's eyes narrowed; his smile tilted to one side. She'd wondered for a long time if his mind had continued to develop, though his body stopped growing at fourteen months. If so, he chose never to speak. But his eyes seemed to understand much. To hell with it, she decided. Let him hear. Let him know.

"Perhaps the time has come to smother the child."

Bertram's head swung in her direction, his face a horrified mask. "But he's our grandson."

"He's not, and you know it. He's our son. Our forty-eight-year-old son, and it's time we put an end to him. He's the Devil's work."

Bertram rose with the child in his arms. "You've always hated him, always feared his serene manner. The way you read into his kindly expressions and playful ways ..."

Adam crawled up to his father's shoulder and pointed at Eudora, his crooked smile parting to expose a ridge of pointed teeth. Bertram moved toward her. She copied his movements in reverse, as if they were engaged in a dance.

"You jealous bitch! You can't stand losing attention to the boy, can you?"

She took another backward step and met with a wall. Finding no words, she only shook her head in disbelief.

"We'll teach you to plot against us!" Bertram yelled, and Adam lunged from his perch, affixing himself to his mother's neck with those fang-like teeth.

The pain was intense, but Eudora refused to scream. She fell to the floor and left him to suckle. Much of her lifeblood drained into the carpet, but she could hear the boy lapping and guzzling his share. If she couldn't kill him, maybe this was the next best thing. As long as she was free of him at last.

Bertram stood over her and laughed, his jiggling form and reddened face her final observation of the world.

SACRIFICIAL LAMB

The rain seemed to be coming down at more of an angle with each mile that rolled beneath the minivan. Rodney kept out of the ruts worn into the old highway. That's where the water pooled, and be damned if he hadn't hydroplaned into a mild fishtail several hills back. It would have scared the piss out of him if it hadn't saved his ass by waking him up. Maggie and the kids had been out for over an hour. What they didn't know wouldn't hurt them any, the way he figured it.

But now the fatigue was setting in again. He hated driving into the night to begin with, and the pounding rain and whip-strike wind gusts had his nerves feeling like the ratty fringe of a throw rug.

Lodging next exit, according to the blue sign up ahead. It even bore the image of a hard-edged little white bed. That would be the Cedar Trail Lodge from the billboard several miles back. The universal symbol for lodging had never looked more inviting.

He re-knuckled the steering wheel and pushed himself into a more upright posture, allowing a little blood to flow through his sleeping butt. It was good to have a terminus. In fact, everything was good suddenly. His fears allayed, his blessings overcame him in a kind of welcome contrast. He glanced over at Maggie, the love of his life: fragile with her sleeping head up against the window, lovely. A quick check in the rearview mirror revealed Mick and Jasmine (Jazz for short) in a state of harmony that belied the nearly constant bickering that passed between them whenever he put them in a vehicle together.

Yup, Rodney Lindon was a lucky man, and when he climbed into bed for the night, he'd feel even luckier.

* * *

"May I help you?" the young woman behind the desk asked as Rodney tripped over the runner for the sliding-glass door and nearly pulled a Buster Keaton. He wondered what it would take to get a rise out of her. She must have been as tightly wound as the bun of black hair at the back of her head.

It was an awkward trek across the expansive lobby. The desk clerk had raised her voice to address him from afar. That wasn't his style, and it triggered his anxiety. A small voice in the recesses of his mind urged him to turn tail, telling her he'd find a Motel 6 up the road.

Only there wasn't a Motel 6 up the road, or down the road, or up his ass and around the corner. If anyone was looking for the sticks, as a matter of fact, he could have drawn them a fucking map, because he had found them, sure enough. Besides, he did like the atmosphere of the place. The lobby actually lived up to the highfalutin name, which he hadn't expected or cared about from the highway. All he'd wanted was a warm bed, and to be off the road and out of the elements. He had to own up to being pleasantly surprised, despite his impression of the woman at the desk. Blond, shellacked wood boles supported a vaulted seating area, and hunting trophies festooned the walls. Taking up much of the floor and shelf space in the enormous room was an assortment of full-sized taxidermy. Mick would dig the wolverine, poised to strike from a ledge near a massive fireplace. The jackrabbit in one corner would be more to Jazz's liking.

At last he approached the check-in desk, still dripping like he'd been sneezed out of something.

"It must be coming down pretty good out there," Ms. Black Bun said, watching him drip onto the counter. She did not smile.

"No. No, it isn't coming down at all. It's coming across. It's coming sideways. I don't know where it's starting from, but it isn't coming down."

"I see." She'd been distracted by a pool of water on the countertop but now rolled her eyes up to meet his. "Do you have a reservation?"

There hadn't been a vacancy sign out front, and his balls tingled with a building dread that he and his family might be shit out of luck after all. Not a lot of vehicles in the lot, though. That calmed him some.

"No, I don't. My wife and kids are in the car. We were hoping to get to Bellingham tonight yet, but not in this weather. My nerves are shot."

She kept staring at him, tilting her head a little, as if watching a display in a menagerie.

Here he was, ninety-seven miles from the best view of nowhere, wishing to his marrow that it was spring or summer. In spring the severe young woman before him would have no power over him, and with gas in the tank, if it turned out there wasn't a single vacancy at Cedar Trail Lodge, he would pour himself a cup of coffee from the lobby's caffeine station—without asking permission—and get back on the road, with its endless patience and endurance.

That's what he would do in spring. But it wasn't spring. It was fall. One of the harshest in recent memory. And the thought of getting back on that uncaring, implacable road scared him more than he cared to admit.

"Did you hear me?" the woman asked. "Will that be okay?"

"I'm sorry, did you say the second floor?"

"Yes, we're booked solid on the main floor."

"That's fine, thanks."

While the woman tapped away at her computer, Rodney heard the door track open behind him. He turned and saw Mick walk in, rubbing sleep from his eyes.

"Dad? Do they have a room?"

"They sure do, champ."

"Wow, look at all the dead animals in here."

Rodney looked back at the desk clerk, half expecting her to chastise his son for speaking so frankly. She only grinned and kept on staring at her computer screen as she typed. When she was done she looked directly at the boy, who now stood alongside his father.

"They're beautiful, aren't they?" Her voice was too sweet now, and a ghost chased a phantom up Rodney's back.

"I guess," Mick said with a shrug. "I mean, they must have been once. Kind of creepy like this."

"They're a restless bunch," the woman said.

"What you mean?"

"They're not always still, the way you see them here. The bobcat, the coyote, even that jackrabbit over there. They wake up some nights. To graze."

Rodney gave her an uneasy smile before looking down to see how Mick was reacting to her tall tale. The boy's eyes were attentive discs.

"Of course, they pose no real threat to people. As long as you keep your doors shut after hours, no harm will come to you. But do get your ice and snacks before ten."

She smiled broadly, erasing any beauty Rodney was beginning to give her credit for. The smile itself was grossly out of proportion to the situation, and it revealed an uneven graveyard of dark teeth.

"What do they graze on?" Mick wanted to know, undeterred by the woman's dental neglect.

"That's enough about that," Rodney said. "Your mom and sister are waiting. Let's go park and get our bags in."

"It's okay," the woman said. "He's a curious boy. Nothing wrong with that."

The name tag on her burgundy blazer read Cass. She couldn't have been above thirty, but there was a vaguely unpleasant air of fermentation to her. Rodney was beginning to wonder who the fuck little Miss Cass thought she was, overriding his authority like that.

"There's a gate through the back." She gestured behind her. "We let them out to nibble in the plot behind us. And to answer the next question burning in your inquisitive little mind, yes, we do occasionally lose one to the lure of the forest beyond. But every now and then they bring a new one back, too. And so their tribe grows, if slowly."

Rodney was about to interject, but she silenced him with her gaze.

"You're all set, Mr. Lindon. Check-out is eleven a.m. Enjoy your stay."

"Is there a pool?" asked Mick before turning to follow his father across the lobby.

Cass leaned across the counter and whispered, "A pool, a sauna, and a hot tub. Open till ten."

❊ ❊ ❊

Rodney pulled the minivan around to the entrance closest to their room and began unloading. Everyone knew which piece of luggage to pluck from the neat line he made of them on the wet parking lot. It was the work of sleepwalkers, to all intents and purposes, but the rain prodded them on, and soon they were settled in. The door to their room didn't want to close automatically, so Rodney turned to give it a push. As it swung shut, he noticed a placard across the hall. He barely had time to make out the printing before the door latched shut:

DON'T FORGET THE CURFEW: IN BY 10:00 P.M.!

He'd never heard of a hotel with a curfew. Then he remembered Cass's story about the animals throughout the lodge. "They wake up some nights," she had said. "To graze."

He appreciated a sense of humor as much as the next fellow, but for something like the story of the trophy animals coming to life at night to be perpetuated not only by the owner of Cedar Trail Lodge but also by the desk clerk ...

"Can I go swimming?" Jazz asked.

She was four years younger than Mick, and it showed when she didn't get her way. The muscles in Rodney's neck tensed.

"Mick said there's a pool and it's open till ten. Please?"

"Why don't we all just get a good night's sleep," Rodney said, closing his eyes for a few seconds. Then, "Okay, honey?"

"But why?"

Oh God, not the whining. His head would split in half and a blood-drenched demon would crawl out of the gash if she started up with her whining.

"What's the harm?" Maggie asked, shooting him a look. "Mick will take her. They'll both swim off a little energy and sleep like lambs. Isn't that right, Jazz?"

Jazz nodded enthusiastically and pushed at her lip with a finger.

What was he going to say, that he didn't want them wandering the halls of a hotel where the mounted wildlife got restless after hours and did who knows what to anyone not in their room? Of course not. He'd never get Jazz to sleep, for one thing. But the idea that something wasn't right about the place wouldn't leave his mind.

"Okay, go. But I want you to come straight back here when you're done. Got it?" The last question was directed at Mick, who nodded.

An agreement reached, the children went about the hurried task of changing into swimwear, and soon they were out the door and bounding down the hallway in search of the pool.

❊ ❊ ❊

Rodney woke with a jerk. He had meant to stay up until the kids got back from the pool, but Christ he was tired. He glanced over and saw Maggie's form under the top sheet. The door was opening. It must have been the electronic click of the lock that had woken him. The bedside clock read 10:24.

"Mick? Jazz? That you?"

"It's me." There was an unsteadiness in Jasmine's voice.

Rodney was out of bed in an instant. Flipping on the light outside the bathroom he went down on his haunches and placed his hands on his daughter's shoulders, staring directly into her honey-colored eyes.

"Is everything okay, hon?"

"Mick's gone," she said and started to sniffle.

"What do you mean, gone?"

Already he could feel the evacuation of tacit reality that occurred whenever life showed itself a little too clearly. He'd felt it when the school called him at work about two-and-a-half years ago to tell him that Mick hadn't shown up. Maggie had taken him to the dentist and forgotten to let the school—or Rodney—know. The feeling had come again when he received news that his mother had been jumped at an ATM, and when his doctor hadn't agreed with him that the pain in his throat was just a passing thing and decided to run some tests, even though it turned out to be nothing after all. We like our pleasant lies, he'd realized long ago. Not just the children among us, but everyone. The truth was okay in small doses, but Rodney Lindon could live just fine on a steady diet of preconceived notions, thank you very much.

Only, falsehoods didn't comfort him at times like this. They abandoned him as if afraid of being found out.

"He wouldn't come back in with me," Jazz said in a whimper.

"Back in? You were outside? Okay, you stay here with your mom." Rodney stood up and reached for the door. "Where did you see him last, sweetie?"

"Out back," she said, pointing vaguely.

Rodney slipped out before she could break into full-fledged crying. He knew she was close.

Halfway down the hall was a flight of stairs, which he

took to the main level three and four steps at a time. Looking to his right when he reached the first-floor hallway, he saw part of the lobby. To his left was the less obvious side exit they'd brought their bags through. He turned in that direction, noticing a slightly wild smell in the air. Not quite as redolent as the odor he remembered from the cattle auctions of his youth, but in that neighborhood. The cool outside air was a relief, even though the rain was still whipping around.

Why in the world would Mick be out in this mess? Why would anyone?

He'd expected to find his son near the exit. When he didn't, the idea that the boy could be in real peril gripped him. Between that and the icy pelting of rain, he hurried back inside and stomped down the hall to the lobby.

Cass was nowhere to be seen. In fact, no one manned the desk. Rodney spun around, and that's when his blood hardened like cooling lava in his veins. The animals—every last one of them—were gone. Not a single bobcat, coyote, wolverine, or jackrabbit stood guard in the vacuous lobby. Gone were the stuffed bison, elk, and antelope. Only the trophy heads remained. Their gazes felt especially watchful in the emptiness of the space.

He ran around the corner to where Cass had indicated there was a gate of some sort, barely able to avoid colliding with the wall as he rounded the check-in desk. And there it was: a wooden door much like what you might expect to find on a barn, complete with a two-by-four running diagonally from top to bottom for structural support. It was painted green and standing slightly ajar. Rodney pushed it wide open and stepped through.

Rain continued to pelt the parking lot, but an awning protected him from the brunt of it. The lot gave way to a clearing that narrowed as it curved deeper into the woods beyond. The overall effect was one of exaggerated perspective, and it made Rodney wonder if he'd gone through the looking glass at last. The sudden disappearance of his son; the equally sudden removal of the animals in the lobby; and now this unusual optical effect. It had the earmarks of some mad, dark fairy tale.

He stepped out from the protection of the awning and was immediately drenched. Had something moved at the far edge of the clearing, where it bent away to the left and out of sight? He continued across the rain-slicked pavement as if walking in a dream and stopped at the edge. Yes, there was movement in the distance. Something coming toward him. A flash in his brain told him to run, to retreat to safety, but he was transfixed. It was more than one thing rushing toward him. It was a group.

A herd.

But not of a single species. Here came the very same animals that were missing from inside Cedar Trail Lodge. The same *types* of animals, he scolded himself. It was a damned odd coincidence, and for all of them to be traveling together ... But the alternative made his head spin.

The bobcat led the pack, a sleek bundle of muscles, teeth, and intent. Its trot was confident and lithe. Its eyes glinted in the moonlight, and its prey of choice was obvious. As if picking up on Rodney's observation, the bobcat kicked into a higher gear and charged at him, loosing a commanding roar that dropped Rodney to his knees.

"Please, God!" he hollered to the heavens. "Help me!"

"No!" came an unexpected reply. The voice was familiar but it didn't belong to God.

Mick? How could it be?

He lifted his head and risked a look. All the animals had parted to allow passage of the majestic elk, upon which sat Rodney's son, arms at his sides. All were still, including the bobcat. Mick rode the elk several yards ahead of the pack, stopping within feet of his genuflecting father. He reminded Rodney of a prince or a knight. The eyes of man and boy met but no words were exchanged. The smile that spread across Mick's face communicated everything he had to say, and words failed to come to Rodney's lips.

A commanding pat on the muscular neck of the elk induced it to twirl away and gallop off in the direction it had come from. The other animals looked from the elk to Rodney before loping back to the hotel gate. The wolverine waddled a little as it walked. The bison lumbered on, shaking off rain every few steps. The coyote, antelope, and jackrabbit were the least bothered by the weather. Only the bobcat hesitated at the gate, which Cass now held open. It paused to shoot Rodney a look and flash its teeth. Then the beasts, and their keeper, were back inside, as if none of this had happened. If any of them were destined to return to the wild, as the elk had, it would have to wait for another night.

Rodney wanted to grieve. Wanted to chase his son down in the rain, rescue him from a foolish decision and an unknown fate. But he couldn't. He stood and watched Mick and the elk disappear into the deeper woods beyond the clearing and felt only envy. The boy had found something beyond the padlocks and mazes of reality. Who was he to attempt to retrieve him? He might have joined him if he'd been able to find the words to express his feelings and desires, and if the elk would have been willing to carry two on its back instead of one.

As it stood, his options were reduced to two. He could return to the hotel room and tell some kind of half-truth to his wife and daughter that he'd have to stick to for the rest of his life, or he could walk away from Cedar Trail Lodge without a word of explanation to anyone, maybe find his own dream. Maybe he didn't need to live another day in the world of mundanity that seemed to swallow everything in its path. Maybe it was as simple as making a choice, right here, right now, in a hotel parking lot in the middle of a downpour.

As if in emulation of the trophy animals he expected to find restored to their perches in the lobby, he let his chin drop to his chest as he slunk back to the rear entrance and formulated his lie. The tears would be real when he told his tale, but not all of them would be born of grief. Some small number would be tears of envy. Most would be of joy for his son. A joy he could not hope to justify or explain.

CROSSING LAKE SERENE ON A DARE

"I dared you first," Jason said.

"I'm not going over there," Timothy responded. "Not by myself. Why can't we go together?"

"Because that's not the way it's done."

"Have you ever been over there?"

"Hell no."

They stared across the lake at the ramshackle Clarris homestead, their voices silenced by fear and contemplation. Twelve was a good age for dares and adventures, but this wasn't like working up the nerve to explore a haunted house or something. Timothy knew there was no such thing as ghosts, but Farley Clarris was as real as rock. Even without the rumors that got passed around by the kids of Clementon, Farley's reputation as a lunatic was widely supported by the adults in the small community, including Timothy's father.

Timothy stepped onto a small, square raft that could be detached from the bank with the throw of a steel lever and steered across the lake to an identical dock on the far side.

"If I do this," said Timothy, his eyes on the lever, "you'll buy me a full pass for the whole time the carnival's in town, right?"

"Absolutely."

"Fine, but there's no way I'm pulling the lever. You'll have to do it."

Jason laughed and gave the lever a kick. It budged but didn't quite release, so he kicked it again. This time the raft snapped free and began to drift across Lake Serene. Timothy knew he'd have to turn himself around to guide the little vessel to its destination, but he couldn't stop staring dumbly at his friend who waved to him from the shore and smiled as he grew smaller and smaller.

"I'll be here when you get back!" Jason called to him.

Timothy slowly turned his attention to the steering wheel. It really was a steering wheel, too. Whoever had constructed the makeshift ferry had used the steering column from an '84 Chrysler. Nobody seemed to know who built the thing, but it definitely hadn't been Farley Clarris. The dock on Farley's side of the lake butted up against his property, and Timothy's dad had told him that Farley was none too happy when it appeared out of nowhere back in 1996.

The sky was beginning to lose daylight, which gave rise to long shadows all around the Clarris place. For every forgotten automobile and pile of junk in the yard, Timothy's imagination placed half a dozen terrible possibilities. So many places for an axe murderer to hide, or a werewolf. Soon he'd be shuffling through that maze of shadows and debris. His stomach turned at the thought.

When he was close enough to the dock, he reached for a railing to help him rotate the ferry and back it into place. It was awkward work, but eventually he got the craft secured. He stepped onto dry land and faced Farley Clarris's front porch. A stand of trees, blackened by dusk, kept watch from behind the house.

All he had to do was collect something—anything—that would prove he had been not only on the Clarris property but in the house itself. First he'd need to convince his legs to carry him into the yard.

A clicking sound behind him, followed by a wooden creak. The raft. It wasn't secure after all. It had come loose and was floating away on dark water. Timothy didn't like water to begin with, and Lake Serene held a special terror for him. According to Jason, the lake was home to a fifty-pound sturgeon nicknamed Big Al by the locals, after the character from *Happy Days*. There was no way he was going after that raft.

"Shit," he muttered and balled his sweaty hands into fists.

Egged on by anger and frustration, he quickly strode into the yard.

No light emanated from the two-story house, half of its clapboards dangling or missing. With any luck, Farley would be away from home. It seemed too early for him to be in bed.

Of course, he might be in the basement, which is where he supposedly performed surgery on stray animals. It was one of several strange hobbies the man was said to have. Timothy hated the idea of rummaging through Farley's belongings if he was only a flight of stairs away, but there was a week's worth of free carnival amusements at the end of this nightmare. He'd be able to ride the Scoop-n-Dip until he puked if he wanted to. He could hog the Wild Ripper until the midway closed each night. It would all be worth a dash through Farley's house in search of just the right keepsake.

He threaded through weeds and clutter to the front steps, where he paused to think about what he should look for once inside. That part of the dare had seemed like such a simple task. Now, up against the reality of wandering in the dark through a house he'd never been in, the odds of finding an object that would prove he'd been there seemed hopeless.

The door was unlocked, which made part of his job easier, but it also meant that Farley was indeed probably home. Timothy rubbed goose bumps out of his arms and stepped inside. The sun hadn't set completely, but the house was plenty dark. Timothy wasn't sure what he kept brushing against as he moved through the main floor. A stack of newspapers or magazines, he guessed at one point. A foot stool or end table was all he could think of when his shin cracked against something in what he assumed was the living room.

Soon he was in the kitchen. Even less sunlight fell into

this part of the house, but the smell of a recently cooked meal gave it away. He stared across the room, wondering what there might be in a madman's kitchen that would prove he'd been there. A small table seemed to have a few chairs set around it, and there was a strange pattern in the wallpaper. But then he took a step closer and realized it wasn't wallpaper. It was the silhouette of a man occupying the far chair.

Timothy wanted to die for the first time in his life. He saw nothing but dead ends. If he didn't get out of there, the man might rise from his chair, hobble over to him, and kill him in some horrible way. But if he ran, he might get lost in the woods to the west of Farley's land, searching for a way around the lake. Otherwise he'd be forced to brave the waters that were home to Big Al, risking death by sturgeon attack or drowning. The way to the east wasn't even worth contemplating. There was nothing in that direction but brambles and gullies just waiting to snare a young boy. To the south, nothing but open roads. His options were crap, but his legs wanted him out of that kitchen. Without giving his muscles the signal, he began sidestepping to the doorway he'd come through.

"Boy," the man in the chair said, "get your ass over here."

Timothy shuddered at the gravelly sound of the voice, and the command itself led to a struggle in his mind. Yes, twelve was a fine age in many ways, but it was also an awkward, trying age. He was still young enough to want to obey his elders, and yet not so young that he couldn't smell danger. Farley was probably harmless. Deep down, Timothy had known that all along. He wouldn't have set foot in the man's house if he'd truly believed he was as wicked as people made him out to be. But seeing him sitting in the dark at his kitchen table, Timothy was convinced that Farley Clarris was a cutter of animals, maybe an eater of children. Almost anything seemed possible.

He went to him, though. Took a seat across the table from him. Farley was a large man, larger than Timothy's father. Timothy had only seen him behind the wheel of his rusted-out pickup truck prior to this. He was even bigger up close.

"What the hell do you want in my house?" Farley had a glass of something in front of him and his hands looked dark, stained.

"It was a dare." Timothy said nervously. "I'm supposed to bring back something that proves I was in here."

"Steal, you mean."

Timothy's head drooped.

"And what made this such a daring break-in, if you don't mind my asking? Am I supposed to be some kind of vampire?"

Timothy wondered if he should soften the truth for this question, but, like his feet, his tongue sometimes had a mind of its own. "There are stories about what you do."

"Are there, now? What's your name, son?"

"Timothy."

"I'll tell you what, Timothy. I ain't got a thing planned this evening. I'd love to hear one or two of them stories."

Timothy swallowed hard before continuing. "Um, some kids say you trap animals in the woods, stray pets and coons and such. That you ... cut them up to learn how they work, so you can be more like them."

Farley laughed, and it made him sound like a different man. "Sometimes a lie holds a grain of truth." He clicked a table lamp on, which blinded Timothy temporarily.

His hands truly were stained, and it looked like dried blood.

"I'm not a good role model, Timothy. I've made a real mess of things. But I'm not a monster."

"I didn't mean—"

"Had a boy about your age once." Farley paused to take a drink. "Good kid, he was. Hard worker. Good at figuring things out." He looked up to the ceiling, and his eyes pooled with tears.

Timothy's gut clenched.

"His mother always thought I gave the boy too much responsibility, but Paul could handle just about any job you threw at him. When a boy's real good at something, you understand, it's only natural to give him more of that kind of thing to do.

"Well, Paul was best at fixing vehicles, so I started lending him out to farmers. Earned himself a real solid reputation, too, but he met his match with old man Welter's grain auger. Paul set about taking the damn thing apart to clear a jam. A big old rock had got wedged between the blade and the chute." He took another drink, a longer one this time. "But he forgot to disconnect the hydraulics, and he accidentally kicked the power switch. Made sausage out of the left half of him." He wiped booze from his lips with the back of a trembling hand.

"Um, Mr. Clarris, I should probably be going. I—"

"I was a vet back in those days, Timothy. Best animal doc in the county, if I say so myself. But not good enough. Jess Welter came flying into my yard in his Ford Bronco, so I knew something was up right away. He told me the news, and I rode back with him to his dad's place. God knows how long it would have taken to get an ambulance out there, so I went ahead and started working on Paul myself.

"Course, I lost him, and my wife never did forgive me. She was out of the house in under three weeks. I guess if God wanted me to be alone, he's pretty fat and happy up there in his penthouse suite, because I'm as alone as they come."

"You're not alone right now." It came out sounding lame, but Timothy felt he should say something.

"It's awful nice of you to say that, son, but you're only passing through. The reason I bring all this up is because you mentioned about my cutting on animals." Farley lifted his hands and turned them in the lamplight. "It's true I do a little surgery now and again, but it's only to help creatures who've had a piece of bad luck fall on them. A broken wing, a severed paw, a bad bite. It can be a tough life out in those woods. Even the strongest among us need help from time to time.

"You sit tight for a minute, young man, while I wash my hands and get you a photo of my boy that you can take to town as proof that you were inside spooky old Farley Clarris's place."

He got up with some effort and limped out of the room toward a back area of the house that Timothy hadn't been to. Timothy's head was a stew of conflicting thoughts. He felt ashamed for having bought into such half-baked assumptions about Farley. At the same time, the man *was* odd. At any rate the dare seemed stupid now. It wasn't as if his parents couldn't afford to buy him a carnival pass. And Jason had admitted to being as scared of the Clarris place as Timothy was. What was there to prove? He didn't see any reason to take up more of Mr. Clarris's time and risk stirring up more painful memories, so he left the table as quietly as possible and retraced his steps through the cluttered house to the front door.

He'd never walked the entire perimeter of the lake, and doing so in the dark wasn't an appealing idea, but he didn't know the back roads on this side. Any combination he took would only add distance to his hike anyway, so he cut through an opening in the trees alongside Farley's drive, headed for the water's edge, and began his circuit of Lake Serene.

* * *

An hour-and-a-half later, when he reached the dock across the lake from the Clarris property, Jason was gone and the raft was nowhere to be seen.

As he scanned the moonlit bank to see if the raft had washed up on either side of the dock, many thoughts swam through Timothy's mind. There seemed to be a lesson wrapped up in the events of the evening, but he wasn't sure what it was. He felt bad for Farley Clarris, which would have seemed impossible two hours ago. What a lonely life the man had—his son dead, his wife gone. It made Timothy think about some of the things he complained about to his parents: too much homework, being bored, hating his old, worn-out bike—which he'd longed for a hundred times on his way around the lake.

Lights flashed on behind him as he stared into the blackness of the lake. Headlights, he guessed, and more than one set. He turned and had to shield his eyes against the glare. Light from two cars bore down on him, and someone was walking his way, right down the middle of all that brightness. He thought of alien abduction and almost laughed. Wouldn't that be the perfect ending to his night!

The figure stopped some distance from him.

"Timothy Westchapel?"

"Yeah."

"Thank God you're all right. I'd like you to come with me, if you would. I'm Sheriff Anderson. I need to go over some things with you. Your folks will meet us at the station, okay?"

"Is everything all right?"

"Son, I'll be honest with you. Your friend Jason is barely hanging on. He's at the hospital now."

"The hospital? I don't understand. How—"

"We can go over everything in more detail once we get to town, but it looks like old Farley Clarris finally went over the edge. Jason went to his place looking for you after the raft came back empty, and when he stepped inside the house, Farley jumped him. Beat him within an inch of his life using a carpenter's file ... I'm sorry. I shouldn't—"

"No, I wanted to know." Timothy sniffled and didn't bother to wipe away the snot. "How did you find out?"

"Your friend was resourceful enough to get the file away from Farley. He stabbed him a good one with the pointed end of the thing, right between the ribs." The sheriff curled his left arm so he could illustrate by jabbing his hand, palm up, into his own side. "Then he was able to crawl to the Steiner place up the road and use their phone to call for help."

Timothy had no more to say for the time being. He could barely keep his knees from buckling under the strain of the news. In a fog, he followed Sheriff Anderson to his personal sedan, and that's when the patrol car parked next to it came into full view. As the sheriff ushered him into the backseat, Timothy made eye contact with the other vehicle's passenger. It was Farley Clarris, leering and stupid. Something in him had cracked, leaving his face taut and nasty, as though the bones beneath had rotated a quarter turn and pulled the skin along.

Timothy and Sheriff Anderson followed the deputy and Farley Clarris into town. Timothy sat in the middle of the backseat and stared through the windshield at the back of Farley's head, ignoring the sheriff's small talk. Every now and then Farley would twist himself around to throw Timothy an icy stare, and Timothy wondered if he'd ever know a damn thing about the world, or learn who to trust and who to fear.

AND A LITTLE CHILD SHALL LEAD THEM

Winter is the perfect time of year for me to increase my volunteer hours at the library downtown, so that's what I do every Saturday. I'm not the kind of widower who needs to rush out of the house at the crack of dawn to get away from my thoughts. I take my time getting downtown, always by bus. And still I usually have enough time to take in a play or concert after I'm done, maybe wander down to the waterfront and reflect on the reflections of the bay. Hey, retirement has its perks.

My Saturdays may start at different times, but I almost always catch the same bus back up to the North Woods in the early evening. That's what Ronnie used to call our neighborhood. It was her little joke about how quickly you lose the feel of being in a city as you move away from Seattle's downtown core. There really are more cedars in these parts than you can shake a stick at. And firs and pines and madrones and poplars. I guess you could say there are more *sticks* than you can shake a stick at, come to think of it.

I used to be a newspaper man, so I help the library staff with a little digging. Sometimes I assist a patron in one way or another. It just depends on what's needed most when I get there. Maybe they're short staffed, or maybe someone requires more reference help than the average visitor. The librarians seem to appreciate the assistance, and God knows it's no skin from my back. If wealth were measured by the amount of spare time a person has, I'd be King Solomon. Besides, maybe this way I'll be remembered for a few years after my passing.

That's how I used to look at it anyway. These days I wonder if I'm more likely to be remembered for a different kind of usefulness, or for nothing at all.

But let's not get the plow before the ox. I was about to tell about my homeward commute on Saturdays. That's where my story takes on coal. For several months there'd been a small cast of regulars on my bus. I can't remember if the sinister man was there the first time I noticed the little girl and the man I assumed was her father, but he's been part of things ever since. Not such an odd thing, you might think, seeing the same faces on my evening bus. I'd agree, if we were talking about a weekday rush-hour commute, but it's unusual to see three of the same passengers every Saturday without fail. If the sinister man hadn't joined the game, I might have come up with a story to allay my curiosity about the other man and the girl. But three recurring faces raised my eyebrows.

The father and daughter were always seated by the time I boarded, whether I got on as far north as Virginia Street or as far south as Seneca. The sinister man joined us a bit later. The girl wore her hair in a bob cut and sat next to her dad, proud as the topmost peach on the pile. They always took the same sideways-facing seat near the front of the bus, while the sinister man chose to sit farther back, facing forward. I didn't judge these creatures of habit, for I had my own regular perch just a few rows back from the lone wolf, across the aisle on a high seat above the right rear wheel.

What made the man sinister, by the way, was a game he took to playing with the child. As the bus approached the stop where the girl and her father disembarked to walk home, the girl would reach for the signal cord. But before her curled little claw could make contact, our loner friend would shoot his hand up and pull the cord first.

Ding!

The bastard, I thought the first time I saw him do it.

She looked right at him, a little hurt, but mostly scowl-angry. He only smiled, like a detective who's nabbed an elusive suspect after a prolonged bout of cat and mouse, a thin yellow line showing where his pale lips parted to expose neglected teeth.

The girl's father never appeared to have the slightest notion of what was going on between his daughter and the man with the yellow teeth. The dark sunglasses he wore hid his eyes from view, and his narrow, mirthless lips showed no signs of disturbance. When their stop came he would step off the bus, holding the little girl's hand, always through the front door, never returning the driver's friendly wishes for a good night.

I had no idea at the time where the sinister man got off the bus because my stop came next.

And so it went, week after week, until we were as deep into winter as you can get.

It was a Saturday in the middle of January when the situation took a turn. The sunglasses man and the girl were seated as usual when I boarded. The sinister man boarded, also as usual, a bit farther down the line. And in accordance with the game, he made sure he pulled the cord before the little girl could. But on this particular Saturday, when the bus pulled into the load zone, the man with the sunglasses stood up and paused to unfurl the kind of white walking stick used by the blind. With it he clicked his way to the front of the bus and disembarked, alone.

It was hard to take in what my eyes wanted me to believe. Had the man lost his vision and obtained the cane virtually overnight? It was ludicrous. And to leave his daughter on the bus by herself... What was she, six? Even the man whose sinister grin never fully left his face seemed a little taken aback.

The scene impelled me to pass my own stop this time. I was transfixed by the girl's composure. Something wasn't right. She should have been rolling in the aisle, stomping her feet and wailing until she was red in the face. But she only sat there as peaceful as a bird.

The sinister man and his yellow teeth soon departed by the rear door, and before the bus could pull back into traffic the girl rose and went to the front exit. To my breathless, mute astonishment, the driver let her go with nothing more than a wave of his hand. I was in a fever to get to the bottom of this thing, but I didn't want to give myself away. I rode to the next stop and practically burst from the bus in pursuit of the child, and the puller of cords.

It was dark already and all of the child's cuteness evaporated as she went after her quarry. Like a trained professional, she kept as safe a distance between herself and the sinister man as I kept between myself and her. She carefully avoided stepping on anything that might make a sound, and once, when the man turned his head a little to one side, she ducked behind a neatly trimmed hedge of juniper, half a second before the headlights of a passing minivan washed across the very patch of sidewalk where she'd been walking.

The man turned off the busier road and she soon followed. Almost as worried about her intent as her welfare, I stopped to peer around the corner before committing to the next leg of my pursuit.

I'm not sure if the sinister man thought he was being hunted by that little girl, but he knew there was danger in the air. I could tell by how his pace ticked up every few steps, and how that turn of the head became a regular thing. When he steered himself onto a piece of property near the end of the block, the girl dove behind a vine maple and waited for him to lock himself inside the house. Once he was in, she emerged from behind the tree and headed along the side of the house, where a towering stand of bay laurel served as a mending wall between this and the adjacent property.

I was in too deep not to see this through. The way I saw it, either a small child was in peril or a full-grown man was. In the moment it didn't much matter which was the case.

Reaching the backyard in time to see the girl slip into the house through the back door, I waited several minutes to see if she'd come back out. When she didn't, I doubled back to a basement window I'd spotted on the way. I squatted down and tested the window but it was locked tight. My knees popped like a couple of dud fireworks as I stood back up, and, as if I'd thrown a switch by doing so, a light went on in the basement. Squatting down again was a pain in the butt, but it was the only way to see what was going on inside.

By the time I'd lowered myself onto my haunches, shadows were gliding down the stairs leading into the basement. Because of a wood-paneled partial wall, it seemed that maybe there was only going to be the shadows, that they had gathered there to cavort and be free of their progenitors for a time. But before such a fanciful notion could take hold—and such things were known to happen in the cool, dark evenings of the Pacific Northwest—the girl's tiny shod feet showed themselves.

If I had feared that shadows might dance in gloom with nothing to cast them, I was in no way prepared to behold what came next in truth. The girl walked not on the treads of the staircase but on the risers, as if gravity inside that basement had shifted and no longer cared for the physics of the world. Down she came—or up?—her body parallel with the floor, her dress hanging toward her feet, *not* toward the floor. The man came several steps behind, equally immune to the earth's usual insistence that up was up and down was down.

At the floor, which was a wall to them both, the girl stretched her arms out as far as she could and placed the palms of her hands on the red shag carpeting. Immediately it began to waver, but it wasn't just the carpet that was in gentle, wavelike motion. The floor itself was alive with movement in an area forming the shape of an arched doorway.

She stepped into the carpet and was gone.

As the man approached the last step, which was lit by a floodlight in the ceiling, I could see that one side of his face was discolored, and it was obvious he was in some sort of trance or subdued state. Before stepping through to join the girl, he turned his head in my direction. He couldn't have seen me, I told myself, but that constant grin of his was there, despite the apparent source of the discoloration. It was blood, and it ran in thick gobs from a dark hole where his right eye should have been.

And then he, too, was away.

The doorway in the carpet continued to shimmer for a moment before snapping back to solidity, like a bedsheet being pulled taut with great force by unseen hands. Through the mere gaps around the window I picked up an electric smell, followed by the scent of something like burning licorice.

I hauled myself up, as much to get above that smell as anything. Joint pain largely forgotten or ignored, I got the hell out of there and made my way home.

*　*　*

The very next Saturday felt a lot like business as usual, which is exactly what I had been hoping for. My shattered nerves needed nothing so much as a bit of normality after the previous weekend's revelations. I volunteered at the library for a few hours, helping a retired neurologist with the microfilm reader. He believed he had a medical thriller in him, if he could only get the dots to connect. Well, maybe he'll connect those dots and we'll all see his novel sitting on the *New York Times* Best Seller list one day. I didn't get his name, but I might recognize him in an author photo. Anyway, I like to think there will still be a *New York Times* Best Seller list in the future. It's something to hang my hopes on.

Show Boat was playing live at the 5th Avenue, but I wasn't in the mood for musical theater. The previous weekend was still weighing heavily on me, so I opted for a nice long walk after my volunteer session.

If you want to know the truth, I didn't even try to catch my usual bus out of the downtown corridor. I guess habit runs deep. As soon as I met the bright blue eyes of my regular driver I knew

I'd stepped into familiar territory. He was a young fellow, late thirties. Nothing remarkable about him except for those eyes: blue like from an alien palette.

I almost tripped over my own feet when I saw the little girl sitting in her usual spot. She wasn't alone, either, but sitting next to the sinister man, who wore dark sunglasses similar to those the child's father-who-probably-wasn't-her-father had worn. I scanned the bus for any trace of the blind father figure, but he was nowhere to be seen.

As the bus picked up speed I balance-walked to my usual seat, careful to clutch most handholds on the way. When I turned around to sit, however, I about collapsed out of shock before I could get myself seated. The girl stood not three feet before me. Must have run to make up the distance so quickly. Once I was seated and she had taken the step up to the top of the wheel well, we were nearly at eye level. Her breath was off. Had she been eating licorice?

"You were seen," she said in an urgent, angry half-whisper, and spiders danced across my flesh.

"What do you mean, young lady?" I tried to sound like the authority figure I no longer felt like.

"You were seen, and that means you witnessed something you shouldn't have."

The driver stopped to pick up a couple of passengers, but the load was light, even for a Saturday. No one other than the girl and the man was familiar to me.

I thought about lying to her, telling her I had no idea what she was talking about, but she would have seen through it. She didn't take her gaze off me, and I could tell she saw more than her six-year-old eyes should have shown her.

"What's this all about?" I asked, glancing at the sinister man, who grinned a little but went on facing across from where he sat. He couldn't have heard our conversation from such a distance, and over the roar of the diesel bus engine, not that he would have cared. Care seemed to have been stripped from him, and with it, worry. Maybe he wasn't a threat, then, but he wasn't likely to be much help, either.

"More than you realize," she said. "More than you'll *ever* realize." She turned and retraced her silent steps to her spot next to the sinister man, where she seemed as content as a badger in its hole once again.

My stop came and went. I saw no reason to exit the bus until I knew where the man and girl were headed, and what they were up to. It's possible I had more curiosity than sense, but that's not a new complaint. I wasn't surprised to see the little one reach for the cord as we approached the stop where they'd both gotten off the week before, but I was surprised by my reaction. I didn't mean to do it, didn't even feel the urge coming on, but before I comprehended what my hand was plotting, it was pulling the cord for their stop.

The glare I received from that little girl is something I'll probably carry with me into the next world. It was enough, at any rate, to prompt me to leave well enough alone. I had wanted to get off at the next stop and put another tail on those two, but now I figured it could wait. I decided it would be a good idea to let the ice thaw a little.

That's where things lay among the three of us for quite a while. We all might as well have been complete strangers during the several Saturdays that followed. We weren't much more than that to begin with.

✳ ✳ ✳

These days things are a little different. I got in the habit of letting my stop go by. I couldn't help wondering about those two. Hell, the blind man, too, though he was probably better off than any of us, being out of the picture as he seemed to be. I should have changed up my routine. Should have quit my volunteering and kept myself off that damn bus. What I did instead was the same thing I did that first awful night. The evening came when I didn't just go beyond my stop so I could watch their interactions as they walked in the direction of the man's house. I worked up the nerve to follow them to the lair once again.

What I found there might be a story for another time, but I'm not sure I'll be around long enough to tell it. I'm not sure it's ready to be told, honestly. Might still be writing itself. It's better if I get to the one thing that prompted me to jot all this down in the first place. By the time I realized I'd lost my sunglasses the following week—the week after I followed them to the lair that second time—I was on the bus and it was too late to do anything about it. They must have fallen to the ground as I boarded, and I haven't replaced them yet. At first it was forgetfulness, but I've got a streak of stubborn, too, which Ronnie would attest to with a single hitch of laughter if she were still around. See, ever since I've been going around without the sunglasses, people have kept a greater distance from me than usual. I can tell that even the library staff wish I'd buy another pair, or quit showing up to volunteer. They'd never say so, but you can tell these things. Folks have all the patience in the world for a blind man—or a partially blind man—who has the decency to hide his infirmity, but they don't want to have to stare it in the face. I get it. It's too much of a bad thing. You can spot the visually impaired from a mile away. Having to look at the source of their struggle is overkill. That's the way of the world. Doesn't mean I have to play along, though.

I've been down those basement stairs myself now, and I walked on the risers instead of the treads, just as I saw the girl and the sinister man do. It turns out I hadn't been spying on *them* since witnessing his baptism in the basement. They had been spying on *me*. Biding their time until I was within reach. Easy pickings. And you know what else? I don't think that little girl is a little girl at all. I'm not saying I know *what* she is, but I know something she needs: guidance. There's something about the world she aims to pervert that puzzles her. I can't tell you exactly what she's been up to every Saturday, but to do it she needs someone at her side to help her through our world. My fear is that she might be something of a scout for a merciless brood that lives on the other side of the veil.

These are just my ideas, of course, and this is all pretty fresh yet, but you won't find more of an expert on the topic— not without getting closer than you want to get to the center of things. Whatever she's planning isn't on the side of the angels, I'll tell you that. She's got mischief in her eyes, and in her heart.

I caught a glimpse of where she comes from, too. At least I think that's what I saw when she led me through the carpet. Her not being long on answers, it's hard to be sure of anything. She had taken my eye by then, but the other one showed me plenty. Suffering hordes like I'd never imagined: burning, flying, drowning, screeching. A horrible place. She stood by my side and laughed while she showed it all to me. On the way back out she said in her cutest voice, "Now that your blood has been read by the void, we can return." That's the kind of cherub we're dealing with, though I will say she had the decency to cast some sort of spell, with the wave of her hand, that made the pain of her cutting the eye out of my head almost bearable. So how does such compassion, if that's the right word, square with her ambitions? That's another answer I don't have.

One of these days I expect to see the sinister man rise up from his seat on the bus and unfold a blind man's walking stick, and that will mean his time as her guide is up. My guess is that I'll be expected to step in and fill the vacancy. That bothers me some, but you know what doesn't bother me? The fact that I might be inching toward a second, final surgery at the hands of the child. The threat lurking in what she showed me in that carpet world was that there is much more still to be seen, and feared. If that's true, maybe blindness has its compensations.

DESPERATE MEASURES

He held her hand in the dark, followed the raised lines of her veins, turned the ring he'd offered up for her hand in marriage. He'd need to wake her soon. They were coming. He could hear them in the hills.

But he couldn't rouse her, no matter how much he jostled and poked. She must have died in the night. He didn't dare go out among them alone, so he squeezed her hand tighter and carried it with him into the woods, glad to have taught her the harsh lesson of consequence. For now he had a silent companion he could bear—and perhaps nourishment, too, if it came to that.

VOICES IN THE CRAWL SPACE

"**A**nything new in the evening edition?" Roger asked, tipping a beer to his mouth as he barged into the kitchen.

Dagmar sat at a small table with the paper spread out in front of her, one dim light doing what it could to make the newsprint readable.

"Not really," she said. "Not tired enough to hit the sack, though."

"You ask me, those folks that are gone missing, they'll turn up in some hooker sting, snorked out on joy powder, pants bunched up around their ankles."

"Not everyone shares your disturbed fantasies, Rog."

"But you've noticed they're all in the same line of work."

"A lawyer, two cops, and a judge. Hardly a group you'd expect to see talking politics at the corner bar. I think it's more sinister than that."

"Course you do. Too many of them damn crime novels you've always got your face buried in. Just you wait and see if I'm not right about this. They're probably skinny-dipping in some fancy hotel pool as we speak."

"The paper says it's being treated as foul play. Doesn't sound like they've been able to make strong connections between any of the missing, though."

"You believe everything you read?"

"You believe every notion that pops into that stone on top of your neck?"

He didn't like that. His beer arm stopped halfway to his mouth, and he glared at her without saying a word for the longest time.

"I've been around long enough to trust my own judgment with shit like this. I need the local paper telling me what's what the way you need another lap on the ugly mill. When they actually have something to report—like evidence—maybe I'll pay attention."

"You asked." She'd learned long ago to ignore most of his tirades, to avoid an exchange of insults, elude the bait. "You going to bed?"

He stood with his belly out for a moment, a sneer streaked across his face, but eventually he relented and downed the rest of his beer, happy to pretend he'd won some victory over her.

"Better finish this sixer. I'll probably just pack it in on the couch tonight."

And like a tiger slipping into the woods after feeding, he was gone into the darkness of the living room. She heard the electron surge of the idiot box as it warmed to life, and she vowed to be in bed before he settled on Fox News. Some of her girlfriends complained about husbands who couldn't keep a television set tuned to one station for more than two or three minutes. With Roger's tastes, Dagmar wished she had it so good.

She didn't fall asleep worth a damn on the best of nights. The stack of books on the little table beside the bed was tall and precarious because of her insomnia, or whatever it was. Thoughts crowded her mind whenever she lay down to rest. Music helped sometimes, but she had to wear headphones if she really wanted to drown out the white noise of her day—or evening—and they were uncomfortable to wear in bed. Books were far more effective weapons in the battle against sleeplessness.

The topmost tome was the latest exposé claiming to pry open the shroud of deception that had been draped over all

acts of government following September 11, 2001. It was titled
—cleverly, she thought—*The Administration of 9/11*. Unfortunately, the title was by far the book's most compelling feature,
for the narrative had quickly dissolved into a wandering thread
of conspiracy theories. Still, she kept dipping into it, no longer
hoping to find much truth or insight in its pages, but occasionally amused by some of the author's more outlandish claims.
As if the terrorist attacks on New York's World Trade Center
hadn't been complicated enough to orchestrate and pull off—
without so much as a blip of interference at any point along the
way, from conception to execution—A. C. Baddington wanted
her to believe that former vice president Dick Cheney had personally given pull orders on the north and south towers, as well
as building seven. A gallery of black-and-whites offered a visual
comparison between the collapse of the World Trade Center
buildings and controlled demolitions from various dates and
locations. Blah, blah, blah.

Dagmar was stunned to realize she'd read eighty pages of
Baddington's drivel. She had the feeling she'd turned a number
of those pages in fits of shallow sleep, but still, eighty pages.
No sign of Roger, either. He'd never spent an entire night on the
couch before, despite his threats, and she didn't like the idea all
that much.

Check on him, said a small voice somewhere in her mind.
Get up and make sure he's okay.

What an absurd thought. Of course he was all right.

But she rolled out from under the covers, swinging both
legs over the edge of the bed and sliding into her slippers. A chill
crept up on her right away, from her heels, which the slippers
didn't cover, to the bare skin of her arms and neck. Her pajama
pants felt paper thin.

She was willing to walk through the dark house, but she
refused to call out his name. Maybe she could live with the discovery of his absence by sight—or even touch. Maybe. But the
sound of her own voice calling and calling throughout the small
rambler without a response would launch her into a panic.

Absence? She paused in the hall with a hand laid gently against each wall, her head rolled slightly to one side. *You sure are letting the full moon get to you tonight, old girl.* But she couldn't help but notice there was no hum from the television's tinny speaker, no gray–blue glow flickering at the end of the hallway ... no snoring.

That's when she noticed the sound of voices coming up through the floorboards. Whispering voices, muffled into an indecipherable drone by the insulated floor between Dagmar and the speakers. Two of them, it sounded like, but she couldn't be sure. In her mind's eye, she began to see dozens of vagrants conversing in the crawl space, huddling and twitching like oversized rats scuttling over each other to make a warm nest even warmer.

Had they been whispering all night, her mind refusing to pick up on it until now? Is that why she'd had even more trouble than usual getting to sleep? If so, what the hell could anyone be chatting about down there for so long? Thieves would have wanted to be in and out. Perverts and psychos didn't tend to operate in pairs, as far as she knew. What, then?

Her next step was sure to be the one to land her on a loose board, which would groan in protest, and the whispering voices would cease, their owners suddenly attentive. That would be bad. But staying put was worse, not knowing if Roger was sitting up on the couch, similarly petrified by the strange voices. If not, he had to be told. The only way into the crawl space was through a small hatch at the back of the house, sunken in a kind of concrete window well. Crawling in there in the middle of the night was a man's job. Feminism be damned.

She shuffled for a few steps but didn't care for the scraping sound her slipper soles made on the hardwood floor. Soft, easy steps proved the better tactic, as she made it to the living room without eliciting a single squeal of wood or nail. But when she reached the couch, her husband was nowhere to be seen.

Okay, no reason to lose it. So he slipped into the kitchen for a drink of water or a late-night snack. Big deal.

But right away that didn't feel right. She would have seen or heard some sign of him as she passed the kitchen. The running tap, glasses clinking as he plucked one from the cupboard, the magnetic *shrrrp* of the refrigerator door being peeled open —something. And what could be taking him so long?

Unwilling to admit to herself that one of the voices from below the house might have been Roger's as he plotted her undoing with some nefarious hireling, Dagmar stepped softly into the kitchen to be sure he wasn't there, knowing there was only one other place to check. She'd passed the bathroom on her way to the living room. The door had been open, the light off. He'd have seen her pass by, surely. Still, it was a possibility worth eliminating if she struck out in the kitchen.

Which she did. Her heart beat a little faster, a little harder, and suddenly a glass of water didn't sound like a bad idea. She pulled down a tumbler and flicked her finger through the stream from the tap to make sure it was cold enough, then filled the glass more than halfway. But the water never reached her lips. When she peered out the window above the sink and saw a slender, motionless figure staring back at her from the edge of the patio, the glass dropped from her grasp and shattered in the ceramic sink.

But the figure *wasn't* motionless. It was a man, and he swayed in small, uneven circles, though his feet remained firmly planted. She wanted to look away, wanted to make a dash for the front door and run screaming to Alison and Bob's across the street. But the man at the fringe of the yard light's range held her for the moment, as surely as if his long, bony fingers were squeezing her shoulders to keep her in place. The flesh of his face sagged, the corners of his mouth drawn down into a permanent frown, and strips of orange fabric hung from his torso and legs, held in place by a mottling of running sores. She didn't welcome the thought, but there was undeniably something of the grave about him.

A wave of shudders passed through her. She was usually one to know what to do when events fell out of line with the planned or expected course of things. Not this time. The patio had always made her a little uneasy after dark, and she'd probably feared this very occurrence many times without giving the image time to gel. But she would have thought the sliding glass door was more of a problem than the kitchen window. They'd never bothered to curtain it, and it was an awfully wide open space to walk past at night, especially if the lights were on. Very easy to feel you were being watched.

Maybe she had been. She wondered if, every time she'd passed by the sliding door and felt the chill touch of apprehension, one of these things had been out there staring in at her.

That broke the spell. It was definitely time to locate Roger or phone the police. No need to mention anything about the undead vibe she was picking up from the man outside. Let the authorities draw their own conclusions.

On her way back to the bathroom she found the loose board she'd been worried about. The screech it let out seemed incredibly loud but probably wasn't. She kept moving. The voices had been inaudible from the kitchen, but now she heard them chattering away again.

Roger was not, of course, in the bathroom. She could no longer brush aside her fear. The last barrier between herself and whatever threat was posed by the man outside, and those underneath the bedroom, had evaporated. Why the hell had she left her phone in the bedroom?

"Dagmar, please." Her husband's voice, maybe, but low and strained.

She wasn't sure if it had come from outside or under the floor. Wanting to see if he was in the backyard, she stepped into the bathroom, but she'd have to draw open the shower curtain first. The window was on the other side of it. Only when she laid a hand on the plastic curtain did it occur to her that one of them might be standing in the tub, waiting with an anxious smile.

"Dagmar ..."

His voice was depleted. The backyard, almost definitely. What were they doing to him out there? She threw open the curtain, sending its metal rings whining across the rod. No one was standing there. She let herself breathe.

As she stepped into the tub to get a better look out the window, however, she was shown her error. One of them lay in the tub, staring up at her with malicious holes for eyes.

She tried to twist out of the thing's reach, but it was quick and strong. In an instant it had her ankle. She felt her skin tear, smelled the horrible earthy, dead odor of decay, even above the damp-plastic stink of the shower curtain. In a struggle to keep from vomiting, she almost fell backward. Seeing an opportunity, it gave her leg a tug, but she caught hold of the shower-curtain rod and steadied herself.

"Where's my husband, goddamn it?"

Its lips curled back in an ugly, mirthless smile. "Out of commission," it managed to utter through rotten vocal cords and a ruined mouth. "Only an appetizer. You're the one we want."

It used her ample hips to drag itself up, slowly winning the struggle they were engaged in.

Then she understood, saw it all with the clarity of a sunrise over nearby Lake Serene. She wasn't sure she believed it yet, but she understood. The cops, the prosecutor, the judge. She'd assumed they were showing up dead for some reason that connected them to each other, but not one to which she, too, was connected.

"We're moving in, Dagmar," it rasped. "Into the basements and cellars and attics and crawl spaces of those who wronged us. *Feed ... us ... Dag ... mar ...*"

Orange tatters of clothing hung from this one, too, in dirty strips that she now recognized as the remnants of state-issue overalls. Peels, they called them on the inside, as in orange peels. Dagmar knew something about being on the inside. Not because she'd ever been convicted. Heavens! She wouldn't have lasted a day behind bars. Certainly not a night. No, she had the privilege of leaving again whenever she made her rounds to the tri-state area's prison facilities. They were terrifying places to visit, despite her freedom to come and go.

But her freedom wasn't why some of them had grown so enraged that it was worth coming back from the dead to mete out revenge. It was the *reason* for her visits that must have crawled deep enough under their skin to make this little uprising possible.

The suffocating smell filled her head, and she thought of apologizing to this troubled, stymied soul for doing such a good job of delivering the medical supplies—especially the solutions used for lethal injection—to area penal institutions. Even as he dug his nearly fleshless fingers into her saddlebags and tugged hard enough to make her lose her grip on the rod ... As she fell on top of him and he grabbed her by the hair ... As he licked her face before bringing her head up as far as his reach would allow ... Through it all, and seeing how it was to end, she wished in vain for words that would quell the storm inside his head, maybe save her own life in the process.

But the corner of the tub came at her far too quickly to allow for anything but pain. And there was a lot of it as the thing in the tub slammed her face repeatedly against the porcelain edge, until her teeth began to chip and bury themselves deep into her gums. She coughed some bits out, swallowed others, along with her own blood. Crimson rivulets ran down the side of the tub and pooled where they met the linoleum. She whispered a prayer against becoming one of them, and before life could escape her entirely, she felt a gnawing sensation at the back of her head and wondered at the strange ways of God.

FATHER DOG

"I'm safe over here, right? Ain't no way them dogs can get over this fence? Okay, good, 'cause I'm pretty shook up. If you was looking through this knothole you'd see that little brown one running in circles like he had a cork pulled out of his butthole and all his air's escaping. He wasn't acting like that before.

"But it's the big black bastard I'm worried about. See how he just kind of hangs his head and stumbles along? That's grief. Grief'll do that to a dog.

"See, I didn't realize that was the father dog when I ... done what I done. Didn't think I'd feel the way I do, neither. It was a dare, like. Denny said I was too much of a stinking yellow shit to do anything half as brave. Boy, I damn near knocked *his* block off right then and there.

"But no, I saved it up for the pup. Boy, I feel awful bad now. Like my innards have run to liquid and want to leave me for dead. Denny ain't been no help, a course. He ran like a three-legged bitch when he saw what I done. Don't expect to have much to do with him no more.

"I wonder what the father dog is thinking while it zig-zags around its pup like that. Doesn't seem to be hatin' the way I would be. I don't see no anger in them eyes. I wish I did, but there's only sadness, like he'd kill hisself if he had a way to do it. Whoever dreamed up the phrase 'hang-dog expression' must a seen something like this. Still, a scared, grievin' animal is a dangerous thing, and I'm glad there's a fence between us."

"Son, why don't you come away from there now. Let me give you a ride in my patrol car. Does that sound like something you can do for me?"

"Down to the jailhouse?"

"Afraid so."

"Well, then, officer, let's go. Maybe I'll say hi to my pop while I'm there. The damn dirty dog."

WISH ME LUCK

There were two things that Donovan Hempel feared above all others, but he had arrived at the Platinum Building, where Dr. Lena Mather had her office, to discuss neither of them. Standing in the elevator lobby, he loosened his tie and ran a finger between his collar and throat. It came back damp with sweat. A short, fat, balding man with a briefcase walked briskly to the elevator and pressed one of the buttons with an up arrow on it before glaring at Donovan for not having pushed it already. More people gathered, and Donovan could feel sweat beading on his forehead.

The elevator announced its arrival with a ding and the small crowd stepped forward. Two young women had to squeeze out through the flesh that piled in around them, stuffing the small conveyance with humanity. Not a single black soul among them. He was the only nigger in the punch bowl, as his father would have said.

"Plenty of room," the man with the briefcase said to Donovan.

"No thanks."

People whispered and shrugged as the doors slid shut.

Alone again, Donovan unlocked the screen of his phone and tapped open his folder of social media apps. Opening one, he quickly updated his status: "Wish me luck." He locked the screen again and tossed the phone into the nearest garbage can without ceremony or hesitation.

What kind of psychiatrist had her office on the twenty-eighth floor? He couldn't have been her only client with an intense dread of tight spaces—elevators in particular—*and* heights. Maybe it was a sign from the cosmos that he was on his own in this after all.

He opted for the push door instead of the revolving one and blended into the crush of pedestrians outside.

His psychologist, Dr. Harold Wagner, thought he no longer needed counseling. Donovan couldn't convince him that he was still haunted by the events that had changed his view of the world forever. Nonetheless, Dr. Wagner had referred him to Dr. Mather to further discuss the issue, and a possible course of medications.

And so he'd reached out to Dr. Mather but didn't realize until he arrived at the Platinum Building and read the office directory that she was located so high up in the building.

Fine, no more delay, then. He had a job to do, and there were no longer any obstacles in his way.

Someone had left a paperback on the bench at the bus stop, but the number forty-two came rolling up before he could finish reading the back cover. It didn't seem like he was missing much, so he left it behind.

The bus dropped him off fifteen minutes later on the eastern edge of Capitol Hill. After a six-block walk, he stood in the backyard of the man he'd come to kill. Ricky didn't own a car, so it was impossible to tell whether he was home or not.

A large cloud bank drifted in front of the sun, creating the illusion of a rapid sunset. It reminded Donovan of the sunsets in some of the old horror movies he used to enjoy, especially those featuring vampires. Other kids used to laugh at such effects, but he always thought they were meant to be expressionistic, not literal, even before he would have used those words to describe the difference.

Today *he* was the vampire. He would use his bare hands, not hollow fangs, but it amounted to the same thing.

The wooden steps to the back porch complained as he climbed them, and to him their protests sounded loud enough to rouse the dead. A stranger would have checked for a key under the rough mat in front of the door to Ricky's rental, but Donovan was no stranger. He knew that Ricky left his spare under the small rug nearby, on which a tall lamp stood.

The key procured, he wasted no time slipping inside the house, away from prying eyes.

His balls tingled with the thrill of transgression, mingled with fear of the coming encounter. He hadn't planned this out in minute detail. When he'd woken up that morning he had fully expected to be talked out of it by Dr. Mather.

Should he call out to Ricky or keep up the element of surprise until the last possible moment? Announcing his presence would alleviate some of the dread he harbored, but it would also diminish the thrill. He continued through the house. Pictures adorned the hall leading to the front rooms. The brightness of the kitchen drew him to it, but it was only bright because the curtains had been thrown wide. It was empty and clean.

The steps leading upstairs were carpeted in shag, lending the house an outdated aspect. He climbed with care, checking over his shoulder as soon as his head popped above floor level of the second story. The upstairs hallway was open on the stairway side, with only a two-foot railing to prevent a dreadful tumble. All doors on this level hung open, and there appeared to be no artificial light pouring from the rooms.

Sitting down on the top step he called out, "Ricky!"

Not a sound. Nobody home. So be it.

He waited a few minutes before climbing back downstairs, where he briefly peered into the dark basement before locking up, returning the key to its hiding place beneath the lamp, and heading down the alley, determined to return home and think through his next steps.

The high was only supposed to be in the low seventies, but he sweated as he walked. Life had been such an easy, happy thing several years ago. His wife had been as beautiful as she was smart, driven, and loving. He had shot to the top of the marketing firm he worked at then, taking the reins of his own team in what everyone assured him was record time. The house, the luxury car, the picturesque neighborhood ... All gone. He and Tara had just begun to talk seriously about starting a family. That, too, was gone. Now he rented a small house for himself—smaller than Ricky's—that he wouldn't be able to afford much longer, as steady work had eluded him since the Avalanche.

It was nearly impossible to believe that a terrorist attack in New York City had been the cause of his ruin, but it had been. Terrorism's most lasting scars often showed on hidden flesh, on skin that no suicide bomber had the imagination to target. He couldn't have known, of course, that the Quat Khariqa—literally Super Power—would use his video as a virtual blueprint for their devastating strike against the West. He'd posted the damn thing about a year-and-a-half before meeting Tara, when he was single and had more time on his hands than dreams in his head. So he decided it would be fun to take video of just about every square inch of the Statue of Liberty's interior. He had been living in the city at the time, and shortly after moving there from Houston he developed a fascination with the famous landmark that went beyond its symbolic significance as a gift from the people of France and a hopeful beacon to immigrants. In short, he had fallen in love with the old girl. He narrated as he recorded, unknowingly providing the terrorists with all the information they would need in order to pull off the most horrific terror plot on American soil since 9/11. The body count had not compared to that tragic event, but the symbolic power of the destruction of Lady Liberty was immense and profound.

With cameras allowed on the climb to the crown, the terrorists had entered with 3D-printed fakes, which were in fact explosives. It was prototype technology at the time, but they'd had help from inside a tech firm in the UK. They had booked their tour nearly two years earlier. Donovan's video had been up since well before that time. The Quat Khariqa had planned each detonation point based on his footage.

It all felt like events in the life of a stranger. He lived in

Seattle now. The country had moved on, too. But a sense of futility still gripped people like a strangulating noose. The events of September 11, 2001, had done similar lasting damage to the national psyche, but now it was more obvious. People were more open about their apathy and lack of hope for the future of the world. There was more good in the world than bad. He still wanted to believe that. Yet it wasn't enough. The bad seemed stronger. Suicides were up. The economy was down. Violent crime was out of control. America wasn't supposed to let the terrorists win, but they seemed to be holding their own, the goddamn sons of bitches.

The distance between Ricky's house and Donovan's was more than he would have covered on foot ordinarily, but today the minutes and city blocks passed in a fog of despondency. He walked through the front door of his house and went straight for the couch, not even bothering to get a glass of water, which he desperately needed. He was on the verge of nodding off when the noise of something falling upstairs startled him into a stiff, upright position.

The front door. He hadn't needed to unlock it. That meant someone else had.

Bounding down the steps two and three at a time, Ricky bolted for the front door but stopped cold with his hand on the knob. It was obvious he could sense Donovan at his periphery.

"So the mountain has come to Mohammed," Donovan said.

Ricky turned to him and walked into the living room with the casual ease of an invited guest. His hair hung long and wavy, and a manicured hipster beard sat on his narrow chin. His tight black shirt and worn jeans gave him the look of an undercover cop trying to blend in with the drug crowd. But no, he was the real McCoy. That was even his name: Ricky McCoy.

Donovan should have killed the sonofabitch long ago just for taking advantage of him in his vulnerable condition during the Avalanche. He never would have gotten tangled up with such a character if he'd had his wits about him. But he'd needed a way to escape reality, and Ricky had been able to provide. A little coke at first, only enough to take the edge off. Soon it was a lot of coke, and a little heroin here and there, to keep him balanced. Quitting that shit would have been the hardest job he'd ever tackled, if he hadn't already lost Tara. Compared to the loss of his entire life as he had envisioned it, the horrors of withdrawal had been a mere inconvenience.

"You fucker," Ricky said. "I thought I could count on you."

"You didn't call me asking to borrow a couple hundred bucks. You wanted me to help you kill someone."

"Yeah, and that's not the kind of thing you say no to. Do you dig the gravity of this, motherfucker? I mean, you don't exactly seem shaken up to find me in your goddamn house."

Donovan stood up and gestured to an end table.

"You see this lamp?" he asked.

Ricky glanced at the ornate lamp on the table, a relic from the pre-Avalanche days of yore, then back at Donovan.

"I'd like you to read the inscription on its base."

"Listen, I didn't come here to—"

"Please, humor me. Read the goddamn inscription."

Ricky crossed to where Donovan stood. "I don't see an inscription."

"It's from my ex-wife. It's small, but it's there."

Ricky bent over and squinted. "I still don't see it." He moved in close, and Donovan caught the drowsy scent of patchouli oil.

Knitting the fingers of both hands together, Donovan raised them high, like a deadly club, which he brought down on the back of Ricky's head with great force. The man's forehead cracked against the end table like a boiled egg. It had probably been enough to do the job, but Donovan didn't take that chance. Up went the fist-club again, and down it came in a vicious blur. He brought his hands up a third time, but before he could lower the boom, Ricky's lifeless body slumped to the floor in an ugly heap. Sometimes there was no need to check for a pulse or a faint breath. Sometimes death was as obvious as a loved one's name.

"That's because I lied, you stupid fuck!" he yelled.

One of his pinkies hurt like hell, but there was no blood on him. Ricky was a different story. The red stuff gurgled out of a gash that ran from his right eyebrow to his left cheek. The second blow must have raked his face along the edge of the table, which was old and rough to begin with.

Good, the thing was done. Ricky never should have told Donovan that he'd kill him for not helping with the murder of a drug dealer he'd short-changed. Donovan knew how to keep a secret. Everything would have been cool. He just hadn't wanted any part in it.

But there was no use crying over spilled blood. He had work to do. They'd find him out eventually, and that was okay, too. But it didn't mean he was going to give himself up quietly. He would take what shallow joy he could eke out from the remainder of his days as a free man. At the first whiff of their being on to him ... Endsville, baby. Suicide beat incarceration every goddamn time. But even capture he was prepared to deal with if he fucked something up and that was the result. For the time being, the unique experience of life after death was enough. Not his own death, of course, but life after taking a life. How many people knew what that felt like? He would revel in his rare state for as long as he could. As with all good things, its allure would come to an end. That was the way of the world. Who was he to wrestle with fate?

The blood from Ricky's forehead slowed but continued to seep into the carpet. Ricky had gone through his own unique experience here today. Maybe he was going through it still. This, too, was a mystery that would reveal itself to Donovan in time.

Still ignoring his parched throat, he lay across the couch and shut his eyes against the capriciousness of life. The messy business of cleanup would have to wait.

MICROPHASIA

At dawn he collapsed in the desert. At noon he died without pain. By dusk the world had forgotten all about him. Now he simply had been.

A heron and a man stared each other down. The man yearned to fly. The heron wanted nothing. No one heard the shotgun blast.

Small worms burrowed into the webbed skin between her fingers and toes. Warm and content, they called for their brothers and sisters.

Kemp counted the bundles of C-notes on his coffee table. A knock at the door. "It's open." No response. He went on counting, a little faster.

In the dark, wet earth beneath the stone, a wormy thing wriggled. Lindsey tried to pull it free, but it was rooted deep, and it pulled back.

He has long known there is a space between the bathroom and coat closet down the hall, but today is his first time hearing the stifled sobs.

Listening to his running bath, he wondered what her smile had meant. He recapped the empty pill bottle and stepped into the tub. Ah, warmth.

The lizard had eaten a locust for breakfast, a spider for lunch, and a moth for supper. Did it possess their knowledge now? Tabitha grinned.

I long to meet you in daylight and pretend not to recognize the way you twirl your hair in thought. You have wooed me in the dark, unaware.

The statue came to life each night and wandered the streets in fear. Naked, cold, and alone, it yearned to be set free: forever stone.

I remain still, not wanting to know if my legs are pinned. Are my eyes closed, or is it really this dark? The gnashing is close now.

The polished bear tooth reflected moonlight as he brought it to the man's throat. At last the animal would have revenge against its killer.

Yesterday, had the sore been on her left or right arm? The mirrors confused her. It had grown some. Green under the purple now. Infected.

I stare into your eyes as I break open the fortune cookie: satisfying, until a horde of black ants crawls forth to carpet my hands and arms.

She tells the stranger her name is Judith. "Uh-uh," he says. "It's Lillian." She gets off two stops early and wonders if he might be right.

DAMNED IF YOU DO

The sonofabitch told me I'd understand one day, and he was right. Not that knowing has been some kind of gift. Knowledge often isn't. I guess Faust's been trying to get that point across for a while now. Will people listen? Shit.

Anyway, this takes us back further than Goethe. Marlowe too. Hell, further than Johann Georg Faust himself, who set fire to our fascination with devilish bargains in the first place. My point isn't that everything begins and ends with knowledge, but that everything begins and ends with fear. It's the universal driver. The prime mover. It saves lives and ends them. It gives meaning to our accomplishments and defines our failures. So yeah, it has its place. Big time.

Fear is one thing, though. Fears can be analyzed, outgrown. Their hold over us diminishes as time shows how rarely they're justified and how manageable most of them are. Uncle Terror is something else altogether. He's less common than the everyday fears that are always floating like restless fish beneath the surface of our lives, a toothier specimen with a preference for deeper waters. He also likes to prey on adults, who never know quite what to make of him. That gives him strength. Children have talismans and beliefs and naïveté. Grownups have hard shells shot through with veins of complacency, boredom, knowledge, and apathy. Ripe for the plucking, because all Uncle Terror needs to do is crack open that shell to reveal the oh-so soft and vulnerable meat underneath. The rest he can do while he capers and sings.

These, however, were not my thoughts as I shuffled into the Subway sandwich shop in Seattle's University District, Uncle Terror's soft touch at my shoulder. See, I had a problem on my hands (oh shit, you'll see the humor in that soon enough), and it consumed me. That's why I was sweating buckshot on a cool November day.

I pretended to study the backlit menu board. *Veggie. Turkey. Spicy Italian. Meatball.* How long would it take the taut-skinned manager to throw me out, I wondered. She'd been throwing glances at me like mashed potatoes flung from the spoon of an angry toddler. Even jutted her chin with each one, like she was lobbing something I couldn't see. When she ran out of patience, or customers, I'd be her sole target.

Cookies. Soft Drinks. Chips. Wraps.

None of the usual make-believe monsters made me sweat when I was a kid. Vampires, werewolves, Frankenstein's monster, alien invaders, devils. They scared me plenty, but I don't remember sweating over a single one of them. Sitting in that Subway, a little dizzied by the harsh fluorescent light that shuddered between the blades of a ceiling fan, I wondered how long I could put off the inevitable, and that was bad. Worse than a knife at your throat from behind, maybe, or a cancer diagnosis you didn't see coming. Sure as hell worse than a noise from downstairs when no one's home to hear it but you. Yessir, good old Uncle Terror was paying me one hell of a visit.

My left fist trembled beneath the table, out of sight. It wasn't a hard fist, like what you'd use to smash someone in the mouth. It was one of those weak, straight-thumbed fists you make to trap a dragonfly without hurting it. Only I wasn't trying to protect what was in my palm. I was concealing it, from myself as well as from others. And why might that be? All together now: *FEAR!*

"Sir, are you going to order something?" the manager asked, startling my attention away from my hand.

Her voice wasn't as stern as I was expecting, but I could guess how things would go if I told her I had no money. I'd been down that path more times than I can recall. So I got up and made for the door.

"Wait," she said. "Take a bag of chips, on me."

Looking back, I'm a little touched by the young woman's unexpected generosity. I could have used a lot more of it in my life, to be honest. But then I guess I didn't exactly go around doling it out myself. I'd been on the streets a long time at that point. My appearance, as well as my odor, gave me away pretty quick. It takes a little extra caring to overlook those things. Whoever she was, I hope I never see her again. You'll understand why before this is over.

The air outside had warmed some, or it seemed that way to me. No rain or wind, which was a little odd for Seattle, but nothing to account for the streams of perspiration soiling my collar and tickling my sides. Determined to find a quiet place to confront the cause of my distress, I headed for Cowen Park. It was nearby, and the sooner I confronted Uncle Terror head on, the better.

At least that was my thinking in the moment.

I made it to the edge of the park before my street sense began to tingle. Must have been something about the speed of the vehicle as it came up on me from behind. Not a police cruiser—that sound I could identify without fail—but something with more than enough horses under its hood to stampede my sorry ass, if that's what the driver had in mind.

Turns out it wasn't. The woman had an interest in me, but it didn't involve running me down in the cold light of day. Her midnight blue BMW skidded to a stop several yards ahead of me, at a crazy angle to the curb. She leaped out of the vehicle, and as she hurried around the grill to get at me for whatever her purpose was, all I could think about was how badly my fisted hand was cramping up, and how I'd have to go on swallowing the discomfort until I was done dealing with Glenda Greenbacks.

She stopped three feet in front of me, breathing hard. Sweaty strands of an expensive hairdo stuck to her forehead and resembled the hairline cracks you often see fired into the glaze of designer pottery.

"You Charlie Galveston?" she asked.

If you've had a roof over your head all your life, and a comfortable chair to relax in, you might think it would have eased my nerves to hear my name from this pretty stranger. But when shifting rain clouds are your ceiling and plunking your ass on a curb is the height of comfort, it can give you a start when someone calls you by both your names. It generally means you're about to be shown a badge.

"What is it you want, lady?" I noticed she had both hands clenched into fists at her sides.

"What have you got hiding in that hand of yours?" she said, nodding at my weak fist.

"Look, I just want to go about my business. I'd take a little money off your hands. Otherwise, have a nice day."

"You're not curious how I know your name?"

"Not particularly, no."

"I'm guessing you've got something balled up in your hand that has you scared half to death."

"Please ..."

"Maybe something like this?" She unclenched her left fist and thrust the palm toward my face.

There before me, in the center of her hand, was a human eye. I don't mean an eyeball that she'd torn from some hapless schmuck's head. I mean this thing was embedded in her flesh, and it was alive. That was the truly unnerving thing: This eye, like the one hidden in my own palm, had a need to blink.

"Are you crazy?" I said, placing my sightless hand on her shoulder and shoving her back toward the car. "You want the whole world to see?" I opened the passenger door and shoved her into the seat. Then I hurried around to the other side, scanning for lookie-loos along the way, and dropped in behind the wheel. "Okay," I said, "at least we have a little privacy now. So what do you know about this?" I uncurled the fingers of my left hand, which trembled a little, and exposed my newly acquired third eye. Showing it to the woman was oddly embarrassing, even though she'd already shown me hers. "I'm about out of my goddamn head over this thing. I thought I was losing my mind, you know? But now you—"

"Cool it, Charlie. I don't have any good news for you, but I might have an answer or two as to what's going on. I'm Eve, by the way. Eve Hurnsted."

I can tell you a few things about Ms. Hurnsted that I didn't know at the time. Turns out she was vice president of a property management company downtown, and not just any company: the very pillar of American capitalism that had priced me out of my apartment and neighborhood a number of years previous. Not the way *every* new development displaces less valuable commercial property. This had been intentionally cruel for the sake of maximizing profits. Eve Hurnsted had been in charge of that property grab from conception to crane-building to ribbon-cutting. Caused a hell of a rift between me and the missus. Arguments became routine, violence occasional, on both sides. The hell of it is that I had actually spoken out in favor of the damn project when the developers descended upon us lowly tenants to convince us that we were all on the same side. I didn't buy that line of bullshit, but I didn't see any harm in buttering both sides of my toast, either. Oh, did I give a speech that evening! My fellow renters looked at me dumbfounded. The developers—I don't think Eve was among them, but I could be wrong—passed sly grins among themselves. And at the end of the occasion things were pretty well smoothed over for a swift transition of lifestyles for all involved.

My transition turned out to be a humdinger. Lost the kids after I killed my wife, of course. (Too much cheap alcohol flowing in my veins and too much bitchery flowing out of her mouth.) I ran her through with a curtain rod, for starters. Then I pushed her out the window for someone else to look after. Did I mention we were seven stories up?

As for Ms. Hurnsted, she'd lost a husband somewhere along the way. Bit off a little more than she could chew of the Seattle real estate boom. Treated her post like she was a general, her mission a campaign of war. Well, wars have casualties, don't you know? On both fuckin' sides.

"I'm all ears," I said from behind the wheel of a car I never could have rented, much less owned. "Well, ears *and* eyes." Neither of us laughed or even chuckled. I stared into the blinking eye in the palm of my hand. "At least I don't feel quite as close to the edge of insanity as I did ten minutes ago."

She gave me kind of a wicked grin and said, "Not sure why. You sure you're ready for this?"

"If it's worse than removing a pair of dirty old gloves to find a living eye in the middle of my hand, then no. I'm nowhere near ready, lady."

Eve held up her right fist with the curled fingers facing me. For a moment I thought it was a secret gesture, like something I should return as a show of solidarity. But then the fingers slowly began to unfurl. It wasn't an eye in the palm of her hand this time. It was a mouth, full of jagged and yellowed teeth.

"*What's up, Chuck?*" the mouth croaked.

"Dear God." What else was there to say?

"Yeah," Eve said, closing up her hand again. "He's a talker. Told me quite a tale. I'll give you the ending first: we're fucked, you and me."

"I like it, but maybe a little more detail …"

"It's like this. There's a book called *Inferno*. A long poem, actually."

"You know, just because I'm homeless doesn't mean I've never read a book. I've read Dante's *Inferno*, more than once."

"Okay, well I've got a little surprise for you. It's all true. It wasn't some kind of fucking dream-journey into the far reaches of Hell. Dante really did visit the abyss as a living soul, and his buddy Virgil guided him through the circles. *Inferno* is his travelogue."

I almost said, "Oh, get the fuck—pull the other one, it's got bells on it." Or words to that effect. But you know, the whole idea of Dante's descent into the Underworld being a true story didn't seem as far-fetched as it would have the previous day, or any day on which organs of sight and speech weren't known to be appearing in the palms of people's hands.

"And what makes the mouth in your hand such an authority?" I asked instead.

"It's the mouth of Ruggieri," Eve said.

"Beg pardon?"

"You don't remember the story of Count Ugolino and Archbishop Ruggieri?"

"No, I do."

I knew the rough outline of their plight from my readings of the book. They were both lodged in the great lake of ice in the Ninth Circle of Hell. Ugolino was tasked with spinning out his eternal hours gnawing at the back of Ruggieri's head. Not highly pleasant for either party.

Their crimes were complicated, Eve reminded me. Of a political nature, with murder involved here and there. But the long and short is that Ruggieri's actions led to Ugolino's imprisonment, and when the prison in which he had been locked away, along with kin from two descendant generations, was abandoned by all guards and warders ... Well, starvation is such an ugly death, especially when you watch it claim your loved ones before it finally comes for you.

They both made each other suffer in life, Ugolino and Ruggieri, but infernal justice deemed the count's suffering to be the greater, and so he was sentenced to make feast after feast of his enemy's flesh, for all eternity.

"That was the plan, anyway," Eve said, "and for centuries it hummed along like a regularly tuned hotrod. But things are unpredictable in the chaos of Lucifer's little paradise.

"That eyeball you've got in your hand ... It belongs to Ugolino."

She showed me the mouth again, this time without lifting her hand from her lap.

"*True, every word,*" the mouth proclaimed, its breath like scorched butter on a muggy day. Its English was strangely accented. Some Italian, sure, but something else was swirled in.

Was there such thing as an infernal accent?

It really didn't take any longer than that for me to buy the whole damn fairy tale. I couldn't think of a more believable explanation. In fact, I was starting to rethink my whole dirty, stinking, rotten life, because if Hell existed, I was in trouble. Eve and I exchanged a look that made me think she was feeling roughly the same way.

She closed her hand and resumed her story, explaining that she'd rather recount the details herself than endure the odd sensation of the mouth in her hand as it stretched and puckered to form words.

"Do you remember a guard of demons watching over the grafters in the Eighth Circle? You know, the corrupt swindlers?"

"Mmm, maybe," I said.

"Well, two of those demons—Pigtusk and Cramper—got bored with working under the imperious command of Malacoda, pouring boiling pitch over the grafters, day in and day out. So they started asking around about a way out."

"Out of Hell?"

"No, they weren't that ambitious. They thought maybe a move down to the Ninth Circle would better suit them. There's a great lake of ice there, for one thing, so they thought it would be cooler. Less hot anyway."

"Cocytus," I said, recalling the name of the lake.

"Right. But there was one problem. Malacoda's band of devils was bound to the Eighth Circle, unable to leave."

"I'm guessing they managed it, though."

"They did. They sliced each other's wings off and fell to the ground. There they found a hole and climbed in. They were halfway through when Malacoda's snapping jaws found the entrance, but with his wings he was too large to fit through. He hollered and barked to rouse the dead, according to Ruggieri. Pigtusk and Cramper continued on, hoping to tunnel through, which they did."

"And let me guess, the first two souls they stumbled across were our friends, Ugolino and Ruggieri."

"You got it in one. They all became fast friends, and the count and the archbishop took inspiration from the demons' illicit relocation."

"What are you saying, that our condition is the result of their botched escape from the Pit?"

"Not botched. Incomplete."

"Oh fuck. I don't like the sound of that."

"Ruggieri assures me that for helping him reunite with Ugolino—that is, *you*—we'll both be spared a drawn-out dissolution. They'll be as quick as possible when it comes time for—"

"The takeover?"

"I guess that's the gist of it, yeah. Ugolino was able to telegraph Ruggieri and me enough information about you and your whereabouts to—*ow!* Dammit."

A spot on Eve's neck began to throb, and she winced as she pressed Ruggieri's eye against it. She had a long neck, lovely and strong, which reminded me what was at stake. I struggled with her for a moment before managing to wrench her hand away. Where the throbbing had been, there was now a half-formed ear. An odd priority, I thought, considering that Ruggieri obviously had a way of hearing us without it, not to mention the weird telepathic connection he apparently had with Ugolino. But maybe he didn't have a lot of say in the mechanics of the transformation.

I held on to Eve's forearm, and suddenly it felt brittle and dry beneath my touch. Pulling away I saw that cracks were forming along the desiccated flesh. We both stared in mute astonishment as the arm, from elbow to wrist, crumbled away like dust, leaving the hand to drop into the console between the seats. Ruggieri's piercing blue eye blinked from the center of the hand, its gaze roving back and forth between Eve and me.

Eve's mouth tried to form into a scream that never came, at least not into the world of the living. Her lips cracked and fell to her lap. Then her tongue and chin and the rest of her face. Both eyes whistled out of their sockets in spirals of dust. Soon Ruggieri's other eye seeped forward to fill one of the unused sockets. Eve's remaining arm reached across to dig the eye out of her severed hand. Once that wet, ugly business was complete she pressed the claimed prize into the empty socket of her face, and the new ear worked its way up to its proper location as her own ear from birth fell away like sand.

So it went, an utter replacement of form, as if I was being forced to witness my own fate before experiencing it firsthand. At least Ruggieri appeared to be as good as his word. It was quick. Eve didn't suffer much. Neither did I.

That's all changed now, though. Eve and I suffer plenty. Endlessly, in fact. I'm allowed short breaks, but I'm expected to feed more or less constantly. Eve doesn't say much, but she vomits a lot. I think our sentence is a greater horror for her than it is for me.

We occupy the very same hole in the ice that Ugolino and Ruggieri used to dwell in, by the way. I can see the arc of Lucifer's mountainous shoulders if I crane my neck—and I smell the reek of his pelt always. He's also trapped in the ice, of course.

Pigtusk and Cramper have taken a shine to me, but they won't give up any particulars about how Ugolino and Ruggieri managed their escape. I suspect the demonic duo helped them strike a bargain with the Devil himself, and if that's the case, things probably won't go smoothly for them. There's always a price when you cavort with dark forces.

Who knows, maybe one day Uncle Terror will pay the count and the archbishop a visit. Now wouldn't that be something?

Made in the USA
Columbia, SC
24 June 2020